Inappropriate Behavior

INAPPROPRIATE BEHAVIOR

ˇ ˇ ˇ ˇ

Stories

ˇ ˇ ˇ ˇ

Murray Farish

milkweed
editions

Published 2014 by Milkweed Editions
Printed in Canada
Cover design by Christian Fuenfhausen
Cover art © Shutterstock/Vlue
14 15 16 17 18   5 4 3 2 1
First Edition

Milkweed Editions, an independent nonprofit publisher, gratefully acknowledges sustaining support from the Bush Foundation; the Patrick and Aimee Butler Foundation; the Driscoll Foundation; the Jerome Foundation; the Lindquist & Vennum Foundation; the McKnight Foundation; the National Endowment for the Arts; the Target Foundation; and other generous contributions from foundations, corporations, and individuals. Also, this activity is made possible by the voters of Minnesota through a Minnesota State Arts Board Operating Support grant, thanks to a legislative appropriation from the arts and cultural heritage fund, and a grant from the Wells Fargo Foundation Minnesota. For a full listing of Milkweed Editions supporters, please visit www.milkweed.org.

Library of Congress Cataloging-in-Publication Data

Farish, Murray, 1968–
    [Short stories. Selections]
    Inappropriate Behavior : Stories / Murray Farish. — First Edition.
    pages   cm
    ISBN 978-1-57131-107-8 (paperback : acid-free paper)
    I. Title.
    PS3606.A6925A6 2014
    813'.6—dc23
                                    2013037871

ISBN 978-1-57131-902-9 (e-book)

Milkweed Editions is committed to ecological stewardship. We strive to align our book production practices with this principle, and to reduce the impact of our operations in the environment. We are a member of the Green Press Initiative, a nonprofit coalition of publishers, manufacturers, and authors working to protect the world's endangered forests and conserve natural resources. *Inappropriate Behavior* was printed on acid-free 100% postconsumer-waste paper by Friesens Corporation.

For Jack and Hunter,

and for Teresa, till the wheels come off . . .

Contents

Sometimes
you wake up and you're living your life
in the static between stations, between the prayer
and the answer . . .

—David Clewell, "We Never Close"

Inappropriate Behavior

THE PASSAGE

It was an unseasonably chilly morning in late September, 1959, when Joe Bill Kendall waved to his parents from the aft deck of the freighter *Marion Lykes*. They'd left Tyler at 3:00 a.m. to get him to the boat on time and to save the expense of a New Orleans hotel room, and now his parents looked, to Joe Bill, small and tired and, his mother especially, slightly worn, the way she kept waving, wiping her face, waving and wiping her face. Although he had not slept the night before, Joe Bill felt no fatigue at all, just the same excited strum in the gut he'd had for several weeks.

After a few minutes of waving, watching his parents grow tinier and tinier—although the ship had not yet moved—he blew one last kiss good-bye and turned, took his luggage cart by the handle, and headed toward the passengers' deck, hearing nothing but French the whole way. He passed some of the deckhands tying down loads and marking the inventory, and understood every word. He passed a pair of officers discussing their plans in Le Havre and picked up most of that as well. It was soon clear that nearly the entire crew was French.

Joe Bill made a sudden decision not to let on that he spoke the language. It would be fun; it would make him feel like a spy on a secret mission, not just a kid going abroad for a few months of study on the cheap. At the exact right moment, he could spring it on some unsuspecting officer or deckhand, respond to some slight about Americans or some clever quip or worldly statement. They'd look at him, stunned, amazed, with a whole new respect. The man, they would think, is more than he appears.

Joe Bill's cabinmate was already in the room when he arrived, lugging his cart behind him through the narrow hallways of the passengers' deck. Joe Bill was a little disappointed; he'd hoped to be the first.

"I'm Lee," the other man said. "I don't mind the top bunk." They shook hands, and Lee looked off to the side of Joe Bill, behind his back and to the left.

He was a slight young man a few years older than Joe Bill, dark brown hair and a knobby chin, small, dark eyes beneath dark, large brows.

"So what brings you aboard the *Marion Lykes?*" Joe Bill asked as Lee untied the gray denim duffel that was apparently his only piece of luggage. He took out three dark pairs of slacks, four or five white button-down shirts, a handful of underwear and undershirts, some socks. The drawer was only half full when Lee was done with the clothes. He threw the duffel, still containing some weight, onto his upper bunk.

"I'm going to college," Lee said, kneeling back down beside the drawer.

"Me too," Joe Bill said. "You going in France?"

"No," Lee said, not looking up at Joe Bill, still fiddling with the clothes in the drawer, lining them up straight and pressing them out flat. "Sweden."

. "Sweden," Joe Bill said. "How about that? Cold up there." Lee appeared to have only the coat he still had on, a green military field jacket. "And dark six months of the year."

"Or Switzerland."

"Oh," Joe Bill said. "So you haven't decided?"

"Switzerland."

"What school?"

"What about you?" Lee said, looking directly at Joe Bill for the first time, then quickly looking back into his drawer. He set each ball of socks next to the other in a tight, lumpy row.

"I'm going to study at the Institute in Tours."

"How old are you?" Lee asked, setting his eyes on Joe Bill again.

"I'm seventeen," Joe Bill said. This always made him nervous. He was old for his age, or acted older, and when people found out how old he really was, they did one of two things. They either dismissed him as a child or they went on and on about how smart he was for seventeen, how mature, which was just another way of dismissing him. He'd lied about it a couple of times, but the lies made him feel bad, like there was something wrong with him for being the age he was, like it was shameful somehow. He decided that rather than lie and be ashamed, he'd tell the truth, and when they dismissed him, he'd tell himself that they wouldn't be able to dismiss him for long, that he was way ahead of the game. He was on his way to France, going there on his smarts.

"Seventeen, huh?" Lee said. "I joined the Marines at seventeen."

"How about that?" Joe Bill said. "A vet, huh?"

"Yeah." Lee stood from the drawer, shut it gently and turned his back to Joe Bill. He reached into the duffel again and pulled out a couple of journals and some pencils, and as he did, a little black plastic rectangle rolled out onto the bed. Lee quickly tucked the thing back into the duffel.

"So where were you stationed?"

"All around," Lee said, setting the books and pencils on the desk at the foot of the bunk beds. The cabin was close, and Joe Bill had to step back to let Lee in between him and the edge of the desk. But Joe Bill also realized he'd leaned in some as they'd talked, both because Lee had turned his back and because of the black plastic object Lee obviously hadn't wanted him to see. Now as Lee stepped by, Joe Bill backed up almost out the door, nearly tripping over his three suitcases that still sat there on the cart. "California," Lee said. "The Philippines."

"Wow."

"Japan." Lee neatly lined up the journals atop the desk and put the pencils in the top drawer.

"And now to Switzerland," Joe Bill said, moving back into the cabin, putting some six or eight inches between the suitcases and his heels. "That's fantastic, really. You on the GI Bill?"

"Are you planning to unpack or just trip over those things the whole time?"

Joe Bill took the three green Samsonites off the cart and into the cabin, leaving the cart outside in the hall. He strapped two of the suitcases in the rack beneath the lower bunk and set the third atop the dresser. When Joe Bill popped the locks, the first thing he saw inside was the red leather Bible. Lee saw it, too.

"So you're a Christian?"

"Well, yeah," Joe Bill said. Religion was another topic that embarrassed him. He was a Christian, he supposed, in the sense that he'd gone to the First Baptist Church of Tyler every Sunday morning and Wednesday night since he could remember, like everyone else. But he hadn't brought the Bible on purpose, had little interest in the subject, and certainly didn't want to discuss it here.

His mother had worried about him going to France, a Catholic country, because she thought the people there were drunken and promiscuous. He'd gone, at her insistence, to see Reverend Dunn, who'd asked him if he thought he was strong enough to weather the storm of the Papists, if he was prepared not only to stand up for his own faith but to witness to the benighted French as well. He reminded Joe Bill of his duty to be a fisher of men. He'd written something illegible in his shaky old hand on the inside cover of Joe Bill's Bible, and his mother had packed the Bible with his clothes.

"Humph," Lee said. He was sitting on the top bunk now, leaning his back against the cabin wall.

"I mean," Joe Bill started, stopped, said, "heck, I'm just a guy from Texas. We're all Christians. But I'm no preacher or anything."

"But you believe in God."

"Yeah, but—"

"There's no God."

"Well, you can—"

"How can you believe in God in the light of science?" Lee said, his voice rising to a higher pitch, his palms out-turned in front of him. "Science will one day prove everything, figure out everything. God's something people needed when they lived in the Dark Ages. Step into the light of science, pal. Science is the only god."

"Well, now," Joe Bill said, "I don't know." He felt funny about saying all of this to someone he'd just met. But Lee was so sure of himself, somewhat hostile, and Joe Bill felt that to merely back down, or worse, to admit that he agreed with Lee, would make him seem weak, childish, like someone who didn't know what he thought about things. "I don't think God and science exclude each other."

"But if you say that, you're still holding on to the old ways of thinking. You can't water it down by saying it's part God and part science or that God controls science. God doesn't control anything. Nobody controls anything, or anyone. You still want to think that there's someone in charge. There's no one in charge. We're all just alone, on our own. There's no force but science. There's no supreme being. There's nothing but matter, and anyone with any intelligence can see that."

With that said, Lee slid off the bunk to the floor, moved quickly past Joe Bill and out of the cabin, pausing to step over the luggage cart. And thus ended the longest conversation the two men would have for some time.

Over the next several days at sea, Joe Bill realized that Lee was avoiding him. Joe Bill had always been an early riser, but he was never awake before Lee, and when Joe Bill went out onto the deck, Lee would go back to the cabin. If Joe Bill went back to the cabin, Lee would get up from the desk, close and lock the journal he was writing in, put the pencil back precisely in the desk drawer and go back out onto the deck, casting only the quickest of glances over his shoulder at Joe Bill. At meals the ship's four passengers shared a table—Joe Bill, Lee, and the Wades, an older couple who were on their way to visit France following Colonel Wade's recent retirement from the Army Signal Corps. The Wades would sit next to each other on one side, Joe Bill and Lee on the other, Lee always sitting directly across from Colonel Wade and eyeing him suspiciously while they ate. The Wades got along with Joe Bill well enough, but they were always trying to engage Lee, who would answer their questions with blunt, toneless replies and never follow up with questions of his own. Mrs. Wade especially seemed fond of Lee. She'd ask him about his plans of study—"psychology or philosophy"—where he was from—"New Orleans"—if he had a wife or a girlfriend—"no"—and what he wanted to do with his life. Lee merely shrugged and continued eating.

One night, four or five days into the passage, about the time the days became a haze of wave and fog, the four of them were sitting at dinner. Colonel and Mrs. Wade had been talking to Joe Bill about his parents back home in Tyler, and Joe Bill had been giving them the standard stories. When she turned and asked Lee about his parents, Lee just stared for a long moment at Colonel Wade, glowering more than usual. Then he shook his head, blew out a high, sharp laugh, and set his fork down next to his plate. The ocean was rough that night, and the fork rattled against the plate as Lee began to speak.

"My father's dead," he said. "I've never seen him. My mother has to work at a drugstore to support herself. She's old and sick and frail and has to work at a drugstore. There's America for you. They'll put her out on the street if she doesn't keep the rent coming in. Put her in jail if she doesn't pay her taxes. She's never gotten anything for it, either. Just a sore back and wrinkled, calloused hands and off to work again at the drugstore. There's America."

"I'm sorry," Mrs. Wade said, surprised. "I didn't mean to pry. I was just—"

"Home of the free," Lee said now, slapping the table and sending his fork to the floor, where it slid against the bulkhead and rattled there even louder. "Land of plenty. Hah! Land of a sickness and a cancer. A cancer called money. It eats you and eats you. And when it's gone you're dead. Or wish you were."

"See here," the colonel said.

"I'm so sorry," Mrs. Wade said.

Joe Bill said nothing. The officers at their table had stopped eating to stare at the scene. The steward had entered the room at the sound of shouting and stood at the corner of the passengers' table saying, "Please, *monsieur*," and Lee was still going on, and now he stood and the colonel stood and said, "Calm down," but Lee was waving his hands and shouting about America and how it robbed people of their lives and their blood in order to keep the rich in fine clothes and fancy cars, and then he said, "And men like you, Colonel, your job is to keep the poor people in line. The state only gains its power through fear. Except in America, you can even convince people it's not fear at all, but duty and honor and country and national pride that keeps them going off to the factory and the plant and the drugstore."

"Sit down, please," Mrs. Wade said now, and the steward said again, "Please, *monsieur*. Sit, please," and Joe Bill watched as Lee said, "Colonel, I know. I was a soldier, too, you understand."

"You're some kind of damned communist," the colonel said now, pushing his wife's hand away as she reached for his.

"No, I'm not," Lee said. "Communism's just another tool of the state. Just another illusion. I'm a Marxist-Leninist-collectivist."

"I *knew* it," Colonel Wade said, ruddy and livid, pointing at Lee. "Why don't you just keep going? Don't stop in Sweden or Switzerland or Denmark or wherever it is you're going. Just keep on. You'd be happier in Russia."

"My mother would be better off there, that's for sure," Lee shouted, then pushed his way past the steward and out the door.

"I am very sorry, gentlemen," the steward said. "Very sorry, *madame*. It is the ship, *certainement*. It is not a luxury liner, no? Some people get upset . . . how you . . . cramped? It makes some people . . . irritable. I will try to have a talk with *monsieur* Lee. If necessary, we will make other dining arrangements."

"Of course," Mrs. Wade said as Colonel Wade returned to his seat with a snort. "Of course, it was my fault, really," she said. "I shouldn't have pried. I could tell he was sensitive."

"He's nuts," said the colonel now, picking his glass of tomato juice from the holster and bringing it to his face.

"Again, please accept the apologies of the captain and crew of the *Marion Lykes*." With that the steward spun quickly away. Colonel Wade turned to Joe Bill.

"Is he like that all the time?"

"To tell you the truth, sir," Joe Bill said, "he really never speaks to me. We talked some the first day, but since then he's hardly said a word. I don't really see him that much, actually. I have no idea where he goes. Just wanders around on the deck, I guess. He's gone when I get up in the morning and still gone when I go to bed at night."

"The poor thing," Mrs. Wade said. "I should have just let him be. I have a problem with talking too much, don't I, Richard? I always have. I just had to pry."

"It's really quite amazing," Joe Bill said. "It's like he vanishes or something."

"This is *1959*," Colonel Wade said now. "No one can still be that naive about communism. Not after Korea."

"A mother would have known better. I was never a mother. Female troubles."

"It's not that big a ship. There are only so many places he could go."

"Not after *Stalin*."

And the three of them went on like that for the rest of the

meal, each in their own conversations, their own attitudes of
sympathy, mystery, and disbelief, until the steward came again
to clear the table, and Joe Bill and the Wades said goodnight.

⌄ ⌄ ⌄ ⌄

And now another week, or four days, or ten days, had passed.
The sky in the daytime was the color of smooth lead, and at
night no stars came out and the dark was low and cloying, like
the sky had dropped down to meet the water and seal the *Marion
Lykes* inside, holding it in place somewhere far away from the
port of New Orleans or the port of Le Havre, and there it
would stay until the waters dried up and the sky squeezed the
earth into nothingness, until all that was left was matter, and
then not even that.

If only he'd spoken his French earlier, he would have someone to talk to, the deckhands or the officers. Joe Bill imagined
them up late with a drink in the mess discussing Baudelaire or
de Gaulle as the mooring chains clanged against the bulwarks
and the ship gently pitched through the night toward France.

His spy game had been a bad idea. That was clear. But
it was also clear that to suddenly start speaking French now
would seem rude at best, make him look like he really *had* been
spying on them, and they would certainly distance themselves
from him even more. By keeping his secret, at least he could
still listen.

On one of these starless, heavy nights, Joe Bill went out on
the deck for a smoke, hoping to eavesdrop on the deckhands
while they worked. It was starting already, his mother would say
if she saw him flicking four, five, six matches before he could
get one to light, the collar of his overcoat turned up against the
ocean chill and scratching against the stubble he hadn't shaved
in a couple of days. Hasn't even got to France yet and already
he's smoking. And the truth was, he didn't even like it, didn't
even know how to smoke, but he was so lonely and bored that

so many times smoking a cigarette was the only thing to do. He'd bought his first pack of Chesterfields—the only American brand on sale in the ship's mess—sometime shortly after the blowup between Lee and Colonel Wade at dinner, the last meal Lee had shared with them. And now Joe Bill was already up to a pack a day because he didn't feel like he could just go stand outside and *not* smoke, and he was going outside all the time. It was a shame, Joe Bill thought, puffing his Chesterfield, that he and Lee hadn't hit it off. They could have been pals—nothing like the hothouse of a freighter cabin to form fast friendships. They could have visited each other this fall—Lee could have come to Tours and Joe Bill could have gone to Switzerland (or Sweden or Finland). It was a shame, but it was unlikely to change now.

It was after dinner, and the Wades were on deck as well, but across the ship, at the bow, and just as Joe Bill started over to talk with them, they briskly turned to go back inside, Mrs. Wade tucked under her husband's arm against the cold. Joe Bill waved, but the Wades didn't see him, and again he felt the kind of utter loneliness we can only feel when there are other people around to amplify that loneliness. The Wades, the deckhands, the officers, they all had each other, and Lee, well, Lee seemed to want nothing more in life but to be alone, and thus wasn't really lonely.

Joe Bill was pacing now, counting his slick-shoed steps like a man in prison. The urge to fling himself into the water actually entered his heart, only failing when the urge reached his mind. It wasn't death he wanted, just a new medium, a new color besides the gray steel of the boat, the grayer steel of the sky. He began to rehearse the letter he would write to his parents as summer neared and it came time to return home, the letter that would beg, cajole, demand the terrible expense of airfare. And as he crushed out one cigarette and reached for another, he heard two of the deckhands speaking in French about the "young American."

He couldn't tell where their voices were coming from at first, but soon he realized he'd made his wandering way down by the cargo stacks. Among the boxes strapped and tarped there, the men must have made some space for themselves to be alone, away from the captain or the mate or the steward.

"He was in the engine room, drawing something in his book," one man said, and Joe Bill realized it was not him they were discussing, but Lee.

"He is a strange one."

"Then Thierry found him in our cabin."

"I'll kill him."

"And Thierry said to him, 'But *monsieur*, surely you know this area is private.'"

"And he said?"

"He said he was lost."

"Lost at sea."

"Thierry said, 'Yes, *monsieur*, it happens. This ship all the decks look alike.'"

"Uh-huh."

"And the American says, 'In Russia, where I'm going, there is no private property. I can come into your room any time I like. And you into mine.'"

"So it's Russia, now?"

"And Thierry says, 'But *monsieur*, this is not Russia.'"

"Naturally. And the American said?"

"He said he was sorry and left. But it was what he said as he was leaving that is the point."

"What was that?"

"He says, 'Ask your captain why this passage is taking so much longer than usual.' He says, 'Ask him about the other boat, the one that met us last night, and the people who got on and off.'"

"*What?*"

"That's what he said."

"He is a lunatic."

"But it is taking longer."

"Conservation of fuel. Budget cuts. Low-paying passengers. I was up all night. There was no other ship. He reads too
much."

"Did you hear anything?"

"Michel, do not be a fool. We are in the middle of the ocean.
And we are heavy, too. And the wind is against us, and it is
autumn."

"It is taking longer than usual."

"When we land, you'll see that nothing has changed."

"Let's hope."

"Your hope will be rewarded."

So in addition to being surly and rude, Lee was a sneak,
probably a thief. And crazy. You could never know what someone was up to. What was this business about Russia? What
could Lee have been drawing in his notebook? What was he
always writing in those journals? This nonsense about another
boat meeting up with them? Why did he have that tiny camera?
Joe Bill was sure now that what he had seen fall from Lee's bag
that first day on board was a camera. It was no bigger than the
pack of cigarettes he now pulled from the inside pocket of his
overcoat. Again he struggled to light his smoke.

After a couple more cigarettes, Joe Bill went back inside. It
was still too early for bed, and he wasn't tired, but he was going
to go into his cabin and read in his bunk until he fell asleep. He
didn't care if Lee was in there anymore. He was tired of feeling
like he was the one who was wrong, like *he* was the intruder. He
wasn't some boy to be pushed around; he was a man, and it
was his cabin, too, and if Lee didn't feel like sharing it in a civil
manner, that was his problem. But when he brusquely opened
the door of the cabin, Lee was not inside.

When you've lived in a place so small for as long as they
had (how long now?), you can feel before you even see it that
something is out of place. Joe Bill took off his overcoat and
loosened his tie and looked around the cabin. It just *felt* wrong,
but only barely wrong, like the motion of the ship had shifted

things around. He sat down on the bottom bunk to unlace his shoes, then quickly kneeled on the floor to check his luggage. It was there, securely strapped just as he'd left it. He stood again and unbuttoned his sleeves, took off his shirt and hung it by the collar from the hook at the foot of the bunk, and when he did, he saw what was out of place.

One of Lee's journals was lying open on the desk. They usually sat, carefully locked, one atop the other in perfect order, but tonight he could see the words on the page, if not make them out.

This was not good. Lee never left the journals opened. Every time he got up for even a moment, he'd close and lock the tiny hasp of the journal and return it to its spot at the edge of the desk.

Had he just gone down the hall to the bathroom and forgotten to lock this one? Or was it some sort of a trap? There was no right thing to do. If he closed and locked the hasp and returned the journal to its place, Lee would know. If he left it there and Lee hadn't done it on purpose, he'd think Joe Bill had opened it. If he just got dressed again and left the cabin, acted like he'd never been there? This might work, but what if Lee should walk in while he was dressing, and wonder why, and see the journal open there?

He'd never been like this before this trip with the lunatic Lee. He'd never had to worry about being a sneak or a louse because he wasn't one, and so he had no idea how to get out of looking like one now. There was no reason for anyone to be suspicious of Joe Bill, but Lee certainly would be. There was no reason for Joe Bill to be suspicious of himself. Lee had done this to him, with his sneaking around and disappearing and never talking to anyone except to say something awful and rude and arrogant, and how could anyone get along with someone like that?

Well, damn it all. He'd walk over there like a man and close the damn journal, and if Lee so much as asked him about it, Joe Bill would let him have it, but good. Or to hell with it, leave

it open, just like he found it. No, close it. That's the thing to
do. That's what a man would do, and if he were asked about
it, he wouldn't let Lee have it. He'd calmly tell Lee that he'd
left the journal open—or anyway, that the journal was open
on the desk when he came in, and he'd simply closed it out of
respect for Lee's privacy, because two men sharing such close
quarters should have respect for each other. That was the idea.
He walked to the desk.

And he wouldn't have read a word if the first thing he saw
hadn't been this:

> *I here by renounce my citezanship in the United States. I take this*
> *action with all understanding. I am not doing this lightly or with*
> *out thought. I plan to seek citezanship from the suepreme Soviet*
> *in the USSR. I have made my desision for political reasons and*
> *it is final.*

Joe Bill began to flip through other pages in the journal. Each
page he saw was a variation of the same theme, the same message,
the same erratic spelling. On other pages was writing that Joe Bill
recognized as Cyrillic, in the same hand—row after row of the
same words, also in slight variations, which Joe Bill knew were
conjugated verbs. So Lee had a secret language, too—Russian.
There was a loose scrap in the journal that said: S. Bulgakhov,
svt emb, Helsinki. On another page was row after tighter row of
signatures: *Alek Hidell, Alek J. Hidell, Alex Hidell, A. J. Hidell.* On a
page near the end he read: *The actions of nations can be easally under-*
stood, but the actions of human beings are unfathamable.

It was one thing to talk about communism, even one thing
to *be* a communist or a Marxist or whatever Lee was. It didn't
bother Joe Bill, at least not to the extent that it had bothered
Colonel Wade. But for a man—especially a veteran—to defect
to the Soviet Union, this was another thing altogether. For a
man to have contact information at a Soviet embassy. And that
little tiny camera, and sneaking around the boat, and who was
Alek Hidell? And now the question was, what to do about it?

He could go to the ship's captain, explain the whole thing, how the notebooks were open and he had never meant to look at them, but now that he had, the captain had certain responsibilities. He could wait until the ship docked—surely it wouldn't be but another few days—and go to the first US consulate he could find, tell them about Lee and his plans. Or he could go to Colonel Wade and see what he thought. He was still flipping through the pages of the journal when he heard Lee say, "I haven't been reading your Bible, Joe Bill."

He turned to find Lee standing right next to him, practically over his shoulder, and Joe Bill realized that at some point, without knowing it, he'd actually sat down in the desk chair to read the journals. Now he stood, too quickly, and the chair fell back against the floor. Lee was standing close, and Joe Bill tripped over the chair and bumped into Lee as he stumbled past. Lee calmly went to the desk, looked at the open journal for a moment before looking back to Joe Bill with just the barest hint of a smile. He did not speak.

"I'm sorry, Lee," Joe Bill said, trying to get his legs beneath him for the fight he was sure was coming. "I came in and the thing was sitting there open, and I know you never leave them open, and I was going to close it when I saw . . ." He was silent then.

"What did you see?" Lee said, after several long seconds passed.

"I saw what you'd written there."

Lee looked again at the open journal, the Cyrillic words. "You saw where I was practicing my Russian?"

"Yes," Joe Bill said, slowly balling his fists.

"I didn't get to go to college," Lee said. "We couldn't afford it. I joined the Marines. And pretty soon in the Marines, you realize that you've got to have something to keep your mind working, or you'll go nuts. I studied Russian, taught myself how to speak it and read and write it. I taught *myself*. Pretty smart, huh?"

"It is, Lee," Joe Bill said.

"Well, you caught me, huh? I study Russian. I guess that makes me a suspect now."

"No," Joe Bill said. "I think it's very impressive."

"Well, I'm glad for that, Joe Bill. I sure did want to impress you. That's the most important thing in the world, isn't it? For underlings to impress their betters. That's what makes the world go 'round, right? That's what keeps the machine turning. Be a good boy and I'll throw you a bone."

"Lee, I don't think I'm your better."

"You think you're everyone's better," Lee said now, slapping the journal shut and moving toward Joe Bill, who took a few steps back. "You're so young and so smart. A little too smart, aren't you? Want to be a big man, but you're always playing games. You think I don't know about your game?" Lee was standing right in front of Joe Bill now, pointing at him, nearly poking him with his finger.

"What are you talking about?"

"The way you listen to everyone all the time. You think I don't know you speak French? I can tell by the way your ears prick up when the officers are talking at dinner. And you're not just getting a word or two here and there. You speak good French. I've watched you listening to the crew. They probably know, too. You're not exactly subtle about it."

Joe Bill could feel himself moving ever closer to the door of the cabin as Lee continued to advance. He wanted to disappear. Joe Bill had sneaked around like some sort of spy the entire time he'd been on board, and for no reason at all other than to make himself feel superior—like a mysterious, grownup man, with his school-taught French and his smarts and his damn cigarettes, which he wanted now very badly. They were in the pocket of the overcoat that he'd thrown carelessly over the top bunk, another thoughtless invasion of Lee's privacy and space. And as he stood there and looked at it all, not just all he'd done that night but all he'd done the entire trip, although

Joe Bill was not physically afraid of the smaller man, he wished
he could take a beating for it, and he thought he knew how to
make it happen.

"I also saw the other things," he said. Lee stopped pointing
and stood back from him, quiet for a moment.

"What other things?"

"The thing about renouncing your citizenship," Joe Bill said.
"The signatures. The little camera. All of it." He relaxed himself completely to take the first blow. But it didn't come.

Instead Lee turned and went to the bunks. He took Joe Bill's
overcoat from the top bunk and folded it neatly on Joe Bill's bottom bunk. He then pulled himself up onto the top bunk and sat
cross-legged facing the desk. "Sit down," he said.

When Joe Bill didn't move, Lee pointed to the overturned
chair and said again, "Sit down."

Joe Bill moved slowly toward the chair, picked it upright,
and sat there. Lee sat very still and looked down at him from
the top bunk.

"This is important, Joe Bill, so I want you to listen to me,
okay? This is the most important thing you're ever going to
hear in your life."

Joe Bill nodded.

"There is a very good chance that there'll come a day, maybe
soon, maybe not, but it's coming, when you're not going to want
to have had anything to do with me. People may come and ask
you about me, about how we spent this time together on the ship
for France, and what do you remember about me, what kind of
person was I? And they'll hound you about this."

Lee stopped talking for a moment and brought his hands in
front of him and crossed them there. Joe Bill, looking up at Lee,
began to feel the strangest moving sensation in his chest, and for
a moment he couldn't place its familiarity. But as Lee leaned
in a little to speak again, as he took a deep breath, Joe Bill knew it
was, of all things, the urge to cry.

"Now, this is the important part. You're not going to be able to say you never knew me. But you're definitely not going to want to tell them you read my journal or that you knew anything else about me. The camera, for example. You never saw the camera, understand? The thing to say is that I was strange, and quiet, and that when I did talk, I was spouting off about communism. Got it? Maybe you can even say I didn't believe in God, but no more. Because if you do, Joe Bill, you'll regret it. They'll destroy you. And you've got a good life to go lead, so don't mess this up. Strange, quiet, kept to himself, communism. That's it."

Joe Bill tried to nod, but his lip quivered. This was ridiculous. He hadn't cried since he was a child, had never had a reason to, and he didn't have one now, and yet he felt his cheeks tighten and his mouth dry up, and he fought, with all he had, the need to wipe his eyes. And then the tears started, and that night on the boat would be the last time he would cry until that terrible afternoon four years later when he next saw Lee Harvey Oswald, on television, being led away in cuffs and screaming, "I'm just a patsy!" while reporters bumped his bruised and beaten face with microphones. Two days after that, he saw Lee shot to death in the basement of the Dallas Police Department by Jack Ruby, and the tears came again, right in front of his fellow airmen in the rec room at Bergstrom, Joe Bill only hearing over and over again what Lee had said to him that night on board the *Marion Lykes*: "It's like this, Joe Bill. Remember the story from your Good Book about Peter, and how he denied Jesus three times? Well, pal, I ain't Jesus, and you need to deny me as many times as they ask."

And they did come and ask, although they didn't hound him the way Lee had said they would. The men from the FBI asked a few simple questions, and Joe Bill gave them Lee's answers, which seemed to be the answers they wanted, and they went away. And he told the Warren Commission, and they sent him away. And the reporters came, and Joe Bill said the same things to them. Over the years, people who were writing books

about Oswald and the assassination would turn up, and they'd
ask Joe Bill the same questions, and Joe Bill would tell them the
same things, maybe a little more here and there, but he'd never
say the big things, never ask his *own* questions: Why did Lee
go to Russia, and for whom? Who supplied Lee with tiny cam-
eras and contact information at Soviet embassies? How much
of his life was an act, a game? How much was a story, and
how much was real? What did Lee know in September 1959
about November 1963? He couldn't possibly have known that
he would assassinate a president who wasn't even president yet.
But he'd known something, certain as death.

And, of course, there was the biggest question of all. It was
there, asking itself, the day his son was born and the day his first
wife died. The day he awoke in the hospital bed after his heart
attack, it was there. Every morning as he drove alone to work,
on his pillow in whatever company house or roadside motel he
slept in as he followed the dry holes and gushers of the west
Texas oil industry, it was there. It's been with him every day
since and will be forever, and it's the one question he has an
answer for: What did you do about it, Joe Bill? And the answer
is, nothing.

Joe Bill never has told his whole story. He's slept and eaten
and lived and loved with all his shaky knowledge and his shadowy questions in his own mind alone, all of this set against the
one true fact he knows: that he's failed, somehow. Failed Lee
and America and himself and his children. He's failed in part
because it's too difficult to keep it all straight in his head. All the
information is confusing and confounding. There's simply too
much of it, with the books and the commission reports and the
evidence and the documents. He's failed in part because time
has passed, and now the whole thing was a long time ago, and
no one's asking anymore. Mostly he's failed because he knows
the stories about the million-to-one accidents and sudden dis-
eases and visits from strange men in the middle of the night.
Every so often, he'll go through a stretch of time, moving from

place to place, when he feels he's being followed, watched. His heart jumps every time the phone rings. He knows people are not who they seem, are more than they appear. He's failed because he was, and is, afraid.

But one day he did tell a writer the story of his last night with Lee.

They were to dock in Le Havre the next morning, and Joe Bill was trying to iron his shirts. He wasn't good at it—his mother had always taken care of that. And after watching him struggle with the task for a while, Lee stood up from the desk where he was now openly practicing his Russian and took the iron from Joe Bill. After a moment or two, he said, "I'm going to spend a couple days in France, and I need to know how to say something."

Joe Bill figured he'd tell Lee how to ask for the bathroom or the restaurant, figured he'd also tell him that most people in France spoke English, especially the service workers, but Lee said to him, as he pulled a sleeve taut and moved the iron across it, "Tell me how to say, 'I don't understand.'"

"I don't understand?"

"Yeah," Lee said.

"You want to know how to say, 'I don't understand'?"

"Would you just tell me?" Lee said as he folded Joe Bill's shirt and set it neatly in the open suitcase, before taking up another and stretching it across the board.

"'I don't understand' is '*Je ne comprend pas*,'" Joe Bill said.

"*Juh nuh comprenduh pas?*"

"*Je ne comprend pas.*"

"*Je ne comprend pas?*"

"*Je ne comprend pas.*"

READY FOR SCHMELLING

My name is Perkins, and my story begins on a Monday. Just as I was about to leave my desk after another day at the international corporation where I am employed, I happened to glance out the window to see a man crawling across the parking lot. I watched him as he crawled—hands and knees, attaché handle in his teeth—from the front steps of the building all the way to the third row of cars, a good sixty yards or so, just like a baby in a blue business suit. When he got to his dark green Ford Taurus, the midlevel company car, he stood, took his attaché from his mouth, dusted himself off, got in and drove away in what I have to assume was the normal mode—seated, strapped in, ten-and-two—for a man of his age and station.

I had long ago quit wondering, or at least asking, about most of what went on at the IC. I started there three years ago—just after Marcie and I got married, just before my father died—and I had seen more than enough corporate and individual doltishness, weirdness, and outright stupidity to make me seriously question the veracity of the yearly financial reports, which show us as a major player in the IC world. I had witnessed fiscal irresponsibility and massive waste offset by arbitrary niggling and concealed by necromantic accounting. I had narrowly escaped involvement in churlish turf wars. I had seen grown men and women reduced to paranoid hysterics by such matters as their table assignment at the company picnic or having their name left off a memo concerning this month's coffee fund. I had learned that the single most important task one can master in business is that of assigning blame, and I had seen the best of the best ply their trade with such a profound lack of conscience that it would be debilitating in normal life. I was even there the day last March when Terrence McNeil—who never learned the corollary to the Most Important Task, that one must diligently avoid blame—came by to show some of his former coworkers in Vendor Support the business end of his Winchester side-by-side. But I had never seen a man in a blue suit crawl across a parking lot before.

It wasn't until after the man had driven away that I noticed the other workers on my floor standing at the window watching the same spectacle. I thought of calling someone over and saying . . . what, I don't know . . . maybe, what the hell? But then, I had done a pretty good job of remaining unnoticed since my transfer to Contracts six months before, wasn't even sure any of the others on the floor knew my name. I could envision calling to someone and having them look at me blankly—or worse, with alarm, the McNeil incident still fresh in our minds—then phone security, or worse, ask our manager who I was, and the jig would be up.

You see, I had no idea what I was doing in Contracts, no idea what my job was even supposed to be. I got hired in PR, then two and a half years later, I got a memo saying that my requested transfer to Contracts had come through. Contracts? I went to my supervisor, who was still up to her neck in blaming people for the McNeil business. She said it was a mistake but to go ahead and report to Contracts the next day and she'd get things straightened out. For the past six months I've sat at my desk for eight hours a day doing absolutely nothing. When a contract comes to my desk, I pretend to read it, sign it, and pass it on. I read a lot of newspapers and magazines, spend hours on the Internet, thumb-twiddle, navel-ponder.

And I got a raise, a nice one. And almost to the day of my transfer, the economy went south, or the news started talking about it going south, and all of a sudden I needed the money.

I talked it over with Marcie, and since the whole country was laying off people left and right, we decided that I'd take the raise and stay there for as long as I could until I screwed up and they fired me, which, since the IC did not admit mistakes, usually meant a handsome severance package in return for the dismissed employee's enduring silence.

So every morning I'd get to my desk and there'd be a stack of three or four contracts waiting there, and every evening I'd leave those same contracts in the outgoing mail. Easy as that.

So while I was interested in the strange man and his stranger method of perambulation, I felt it was best, given what I thought was a tenuous grasp on my frankly embarrassing income, to simply let the matter pass without comment. Apparently the others on my side of the floor felt the same, because no one said a word about it. They simply turned from the window and left for the day, moving silently out of the hallway and into the elevator.

When I got home to Marcie, I told her about the man and how he crawled across the parking lot. Marcie is a painter. Her work was just beginning to appear in some of the smaller local galleries. I told her she should paint that, get a mental image of what I was talking about, and paint the man crawling across the parking lot. I advanced the themes of abjection, endurance, possibly even protest. She said if she painted it, she wouldn't show the man at all.

"But, Marcie," I said. "That's the whole thing about the painting."

"Nope," she said. "The whole thing about the painting is you."

"Me?"

"Yes," she said. "You. Standing there watching him."

She started that very night.

The rest of the week passed without incident. Every day at a little before five, I would peer out the window, looking for the man to crawl across the parking lot, but he never did. I thought I caught a glimpse of him one day, walking normally, and I tried to follow him with my eyes all the way to his car, to see if it was the same man. But there were lots of men in blue suits and lots of dark green Ford Tauruses, so I wasn't sure.

That Friday night when I got home from the office, Marcie was very glad to see me. She met me at the door and kissed me deeply, her arms around my neck and her tongue dabbing madly in my mouth. Before I could even get a word out, she was taking off her clothes, and then she took off mine, and we made love there on the living room floor. After, both of us still unclothed, she took my hand and led me to the spare bedroom that served as her studio. There on the easel was the sketch of the painting we had talked about. I was standing at the window in coat and tie, with a look on my face that was a mix of revulsion and pity and confusion and, I thought, just the barest hint of shame. I thought of mentioning to Marcie that revulsion and confusion were right on the money, and that pity was good—I should have felt pity somehow, I thought, and it made me feel a little bad that I hadn't—but I had not been ashamed. Instead we got dressed and went out for drinks and a steak dinner, which is what we always did on Fridays after Marcie had a good week of work. When we got home, we made love again, this time on the floor in the studio, with me on top, a reversal of our earlier interlude. I rubbed my knees raw from bracing against the canvas drop cloths on the floor of the studio. I was a little drunk, but more than a little preoccupied as well. Every time I looked up from Marcie as I moved above her, I saw the sketch of me standing there in the window. It was really good; even I wasn't sure what I was looking at anymore.

When I got to the IC Monday morning, there was something that seemed a bit out of drawing, off-kilter, something imperceptible that nonetheless made me want to fix it, like in school when the teacher would leave that one little scratch of chalk on the blackboard after she erased it; if you're like me, your whole day was ruined. That little chalk mark would distract us to the edge of madness. The IC was like that on Monday morning, except I couldn't find the chalk mark to erase. I looked for it, all the way in from the parking lot, up the concrete steps and through the huge glass doors, through the marble-floored lobby past the PR office where I used to work, up the elevator to seven, all the way to my desk by the back corner near the window, I looked for it, but was unable to locate the problem.

Everything seemed to be in order to the untrained eye: The people I saw every day were moving about in their everyday fashion; there was a stack of contracts on my desk awaiting my careful vetting; there was nothing different about the decor. Everything was as I had left it Friday, except that it wasn't. It was as if something as implacable and yet imperceptible as a bump in the orbit of the Earth had nudged everything slightly aslant, and it was going to stay that way.

I tried to work through it, but all day my timing was just a bit off. Where before I had carefully observed my coworkers' movements, and scheduled mine, to avoid even the most light-hearted banter, I was now running into them every time I left my desk: at the coffee machine, in the restroom, at the copier. There was one man in particular—call him Smith—who kept asking me, each time we met, how I was doing, as if I had some-how changed in the thirty minutes since I'd run into him last. Smith was an unsightly fellow, short and squat, a heavy sweater with a thinning blond comb-over, tiny black eyes that made him look sort of prurient behind his thick, black-plastic-framed glasses, a puffy dewlap above his collar. Fine, Smith, and you? I'd reply, and each time he answered the same.

And it wasn't just Smith. The manager—a gray-haired, slump-shouldered man of sixty or so—seemed to be lurking around quite a bit that day. Remember, now, I'd never met this man, didn't even know his name. I'd watch him walk to his car in the afternoons—I always tried to stay huddled in my cubicle until I was sure he'd left for the day. He parked in the first row, drove the more prestigious company car, the blue Lincoln, and his hunch-rolled stroll to his automobile was usually all I saw of him. Today he was wandering around seven like some kind of golem, never stopping to speak or even so much as look at anyone, his face an attitude of profound confusion. I tried to avoid his gaze, stayed crouched over the papers on my desk in what I hoped passed for intense concentration, and when he started to get too close, I'd skulk away to the bathroom, walking a little bent-kneed to stay below cubicle level. My evasive maneuvers were effective if belittling, and I made it through the end of the day, still employed, but no closer to finding that overlooked chalk mark.

Just as I was about to leave my desk—while watching the manager slumping along to his car, head down, feet like clay—I heard a sound from outside my cubicle. It was Smith, and he was, for some reason, saying, "Psst," and peeking over the top of the partition.

"How're you doing, Smith?"

"Fine, and you?"

"Another day."

"Not quite yet," Smith said.

"Smith," I said, suddenly aware that he had to be standing on his tiptoes, "would you like to come into my cubicle?"

"Thanks," he said, his head and neck—which were one piece—then the rest of him appearing from behind the partition. "Are you ready?"

"Yes," I said. "All done. So . . . I guess I'll see you tomorrow."

"No, no, no," Smith said, then peered furtively back behind the partition. He turned back toward me, leaned in close, and, barely whispering, said, "Are you ready for Schmelling?"

The only thing I could think to say was, I don't know, at which point Smith put his hands on my shoulders and whisked me from my chair. We moved together like dance partners toward the window, where we stopped and, lacking much space in the cubicle, stood very close. I could smell Smith next to me; just above his sweat were the odors of cigarette smoke and Brut aftershave. Up close, I could see that he had had a terrible acne problem, and had some sort of wen on his nose as well, up near the inner canthus of his left eye, causing his black frames to rest slightly crooked on what passed for the bridge of his pug nose. He was a thoroughly unattractive man, but I soon saw that something amazing was happening to his face. He was glowing, turning a healthy, sanguine scarlet, his eyes gleaming like tiny black pearls behind his glasses, his lips trembling in what can only be described—or at least I saw it this way, and still believe it true—as the paroxysms of rapture. I wanted to see what was exciting him so, but I was so transfixed by the bliss on his face I was unable to turn my attention. His breathing was coming a little heavier now, starting to fog the window in front of him. He made a quick, jerking motion with his right arm, grabbed his graying shirt sleeve in his palm and wiped away the condensation. It was then that he said, in a gasp and a squeal, "There he is."

I looked out the window, down into the parking lot, where the man who had crawled to his car the previous Monday was this Monday doing a perfect phys. ed. crabwalk across the parking lot: his arms directly perpendicular to the ground, his knees bent at T-square-grade right angles, kicking forward on cue to propel himself to his car like some sort of Cossack dancer. Whereas the week before he carried his attaché case in his teeth, today it rested on his perfectly flat chest, at no point threatening to upend. When he got to the third row, to his dark green Ford Taurus, he bent his arms a bit, and then, all in one motion, sprung to his feet and caught the attaché between both hands. He pirouetted to face the building, raised the attaché above his head like a championship belt, and offered the slightest of bows. With that he turned again, unlocked his car, got in and drove away.

I stood and continued to stare out the window, having no idea at all what to make of this. Just as I was about to turn and ask Smith . . . what, I don't know . . . he took an audibly deep breath and expelled that breath with, "God, I admire him." He stood in reverie just a second more, then turned, patted me on the back and said, "Well, see you tomorrow." And with that he was gone.

Maybe now would be the time, in a quick hundred words or so, to explain something to you, about me. I am a simple man, basically, in terms of how I view the world. I do not believe the world is a confusing place, so long as one does not unnecessarily complicate one's view of it. I do not believe in UFOs, Bigfoot, angels, mysticism, magic, channeling, that there was a second shooter on the grassy knoll, or that 9-11 was an inside job. I do not believe that there are any underlying mysteries. I do not believe in looking either above or below the surface of things, because I think there's more than enough on the surface to keep us occupied for the length of any one life, which, I believe, is all we get. I do not believe in God. I do not believe in heaven. I do not believe in hell. I believe that life is this world alone, is what we make of it, each to his own abilities and needs.

Knowing all of this about myself, I can, I think, be forgiven for a moment of stuporous inactivity, a stunned paralysis of movement and speech, even of thought. I find it hard, however, to let myself off the hook, for by the time I was able to move, Smith, along with the rest of the seventh floor, was gone, and I was left all alone. I knew I should do something, that seemed clear. But what? How does one react to a grown man crab-walking across a parking lot with an attaché on his chest, especially when that man, or his actions, have apparently inspired some sort of cult following among the people with whom one works? I thought at first to move, quickly, to flee, to get out of that building, use my sick time for a few days until I figured out what to do, or figured out a way to never go back. But then I caught sight of Smith, walking, as normally as Smith could, across the parking lot to his car. I saw him get into a gray Saturn, and as soon as he did I sprinted from my desk down the seven flights of stairs and made it to the parking lot just in time to see him drive away. He turned left out of the parking lot and I ran madly to my car to tail him.

When I got onto the access road, I could see Smith's car heading west on the highway, so I floored it and jumped two lanes of traffic to follow him. Just as I hit the highway, my cell phone rang. It was Marcie.

"When are you coming home?" she said as I wrenched my neck to hold the phone while keeping both hands on the wheel. I was doing nearly eighty, and Smith was still well down the road. The late September sun hung blandly in my windshield, and I reached up with my left hand to lower the visor, dropping the phone from my neck as I did. I managed to shift my hips and catch it in my lap, but not before swerving into the service lane, then swerving out against an angry, guttural horn blast from a semi to my left.

"I'm just going out for a quick drink with some friends," I shouted into my lap as Smith began a rightward move across traffic, some quarter mile ahead of me.

"Friends?" Marcie's voice came from the phone, dubiously.

"Some of the guys from work."

"I wish you'd come home," she said. "I have something incredible to show you."

I saw Smith exit onto Dunleavy. I swerved, said to Marcie, "I won't be late," then flipped the phone closed while executing a nifty move between a school bus full of band members and an SUV. I had to hurry, or Smith would get lost in side streets.

When I got to the top of the exit onto Dunleavy, I saw Smith's car turn into a strip mall six blocks down the road. At least he wasn't going home yet. As badly as I wanted some answers, I wanted no part of Smith's home life. There are things in this world you just can't get out of your head, and Smith's house, I knew, would be one of them.

His car was parked in front of a Walgreens, so I parked nearby and went inside. I could imagine catching Smith in an aisle where you'd rather not be caught, perhaps foot care or fungicides or protective undergarments. But a fairly good look around the place brought no sign of Smith. I was approached by a retarded boy in a blue smock who asked me if he could help me find anything. When I told him no, he moved on to someone else, a woman who said, "Yes, cough syrup," at which point the retarded boy called someone to help the woman find cough syrup.

I left Walgreens thinking Smith must be in another of the shops in the strip mall. But when I got to the parking lot, the gray Saturn was gone.

Not knowing what else to do, I went home. On the way, now driving with the last of the sun at my back, I thought about how silly all of this was. That I would go chasing after Smith like some sort of madman, as if Smith had any answers, as if the incident I had witnessed even merited answers. I realized now that Schmelling's antics in the parking lot were nothing more than that, antics, some sort of frat prank that he and his acolytes never outgrew, a symbolic thumbing of the nose at the IC and the conformity it bred, and if Smith and some of the others were a bit carried away by the whole thing, that was their problem, not mine.

When I got home, Marcie was again very glad to see me. She met me at the door, already unclothed, and the next thing I knew, she was on her knees in front of me. When she finished, as I hung there, leaning against the front door to support my shaky legs, she took me by my limpening member and led me to the studio. There was the sketch, but now a full painting, finished and beautiful, maybe her best work yet. My face and white shirt were colored by the setting sun through the glass of the window, which she had somehow portrayed without showing any glass at all. My tie was an iridescent stripe of blues and greens and reds woven together to produce an effect of color the likes of which I'd never seen. My hand against the window-pane was the picture's most stunning feature. I seemed from one angle to be waving; from another, I held up my hand as if to say, Stop! From still another, I was a startled man bracing himself against the glass, which, as I've said, was both there and

not there at once, which led to an even more eerie effect, that of
a man trying not to fall as the building behind him leaned. I was
completely carried away by the painting, so much so that I
hadn't noticed Marcie's hand moving on me, working me back
to a state of arousal. Before I could speak, Marcie dragged me to
the ground and climbed on top of me, inserting me into her
as I became fully hard again. This may have been the single—or
double, or triple, I lost count—greatest sexual experience of our
marriage, and by the time we were done, even the palms of my
hands and the soles of my feet were tender from pushing against
the canvas drop cloths.

After, lying together on the floor beneath the easel, beneath
the painting that could very well be the best American portrait
since *Whistler's Mother*, I told her about Schmelling, that today,
instead of crawling, he crabwalked, told her I'd figured it all out,
that he was some poor midlevel schmuck who was never going
anywhere and that his way of rebelling was to put on this weird
act in the parking lot every so often. I wanted to tell her about
following Smith, about the way things seemed out of place at
the IC that day, about having to avoid the manager, about the
retarded boy at Walgreens, but I never got the chance. As soon
as I got it out about Schmelling and the crabwalk, she leaped to
her feet as if someone had poked her with a cattle prod. I tried
to call for her, but she was already gone from the room. She'd
run into our bedroom and locked the door, and standing there
in the hallway, naked and cold and covered with the sticky, dry-
ing liquids of our love, I could hear her crying.

After trying the door and calling for her a couple of times,
I, not knowing what else to do, went to the guest bathroom
to take a shower. While I was in there, lathering and rinsing
and trying to guess what in the world I'd done wrong, I could
hear her stomping about outside in the hall between our bedroom and the studio. I wasn't that alarmed, really, at least not
as alarmed as I realize now I should have been. I mean, I lived
with Marcie, she was my wife, and she was temperamental, and

much more of a believer, or at least much more receptive, to the things in life that float beneath the surface (which, as I said before, we create for ourselves as need be). Marcie was the artist, the woman of moods and funks and elations, and I was the calm, levelheaded one who kept us grounded in the world and made the work she did possible. It was the perfect arrangement, it seemed to me, each of us using our own skills and bents and frames of mind to make our marriage a true union, to make up one body that was prepared to meet the world on whatever terms it asked of us. I still had no idea what I'd done wrong, but I decided it didn't matter—I'd get out of the shower, towel off, and then go to her and hold her until she calmed down, and I'd say I'm sorry and I'm sorry and I'm sorry again, for whatever I'd done to upset her. And then the door opened, and she flung back the shower curtain and threw in the painting in six neatly razored, beautifully colored strips.

I jumped quickly to dodge the initial burst of whatever she was throwing at me, but when I saw it was the painting and that it was being ruined by the water, I tried to pick it up somehow. She stood there, tiny and furious, wreathed by steam.

"Just *leave* it," Marcie said. "You're the one who *killed* it."

"Marcie, what are you talking about? I thought—"

"No, you *didn't* think, you son of a bitch. You didn't think at all."

"What are you . . . why did you do this?"

"I could ask you the same thing, couldn't I?" She was really screaming now, trying to talk through the kind of tears that should be saved for those two or three times in your life when unless you cry like that there's no way to go on living, the kind of tears that leave you completely at their mercy, when you can't even control your arms and legs and spine anymore, so you flail around in some kind of rhythm that only your sobbing knows. "You . . . *murderer!*"

When I stepped out of the shower, she got control of herself enough to run from the bathroom. She returned to the bedroom and locked the door and stayed in there and cried all night long. I lay on the couch and watched a show on Animal Planet about otters and their lives until I fell asleep. When I awoke the next morning, early, she was already in the studio, with that door locked as well. I figured it would be best to leave things be for a while, to go on in to work and give her some peace, and then, when we'd had a chance to clear our heads, talk about it tonight.

So I got dressed and drove to the office. As I started down the access road, I looked about to try to see the thing that had bothered me the day before, the missed chalk mark. But I couldn't find it again, and as I approached the IC, as I pulled into my parking space, as I went through the huge glass doors and across the marble-floored lobby past PR and into the elevator, it seemed that someone else had found it and erased it unequivocally. Everything was in order, the way it had always been, as though during the night, fearing discovery by my wary eye, whoever or whatever had shifted things had come and shifted them back, sighing with relief over the closeness of the call, determined never to try to sneak anything past me again. The elevator disgorged several women from Marketing onto three, a janitor got off on four, and I was alone and feeling fine up to seven. I looked down at my tie, which was, coincidentally, the same tie I had worn in Marcie's picture. I was straightening it in the shiny brass reflection of the elevator keypad just as the bell for seven rang. I reached down for my briefcase, and when I looked up, I was staring straight into the blank and pitiless face of the manager.

My heart stopped—I really believe it did—for just a second, and then it began to move about wildly in my chest like some sort of little swamp mammal trapped in an underwater tree trunk. The manager was a bit taller than I, and he looked down at me with baggy, red-rimmed, jaundiced eyes that registered nothing about who I was or what I might be doing there in the elevator, much less attempting to get off on his floor. I was so riveted with fear that until I was shoved aside by them,

I didn't even notice the IC security guards at the manager's elbows, accompanying him like escorts at a pageant or a dance. They moved by me and brought the manager into the elevator. I turned, still looking into the yellow sclera of the manager's eyes, our gazes locked, until one of the guards said, "Getting off, Mr. Perkins?"

Hearing my name snapped the spell the old man had on me. I looked back and forth quickly at the two other men to ascertain which of them had said it, which of them knew who I was, although it could hardly matter. If one of them knew me, the other did, too, and everyone else on seven as well, and everyone in the entire IC, and that meant that this otherwise unremarkable Tuesday was to be, no doubt, my last in the employ of this prestigious concern, and that tonight, instead of patching things up with Marcie, I would spend the evening updating my résumé, making phone calls, and trying to figure out how to keep paying our mortgage on nothing more than an unemployment check.

I moved from the elevator, down the hall to the main room of the floor, and toward my desk in the corner near the window. It seemed to take forever to get there, as if this morning I were the one with feet of clay, but the time it took me to get there allowed me to notice a rather strange thing. Everyone on the floor was looking out from behind their cubicle partitions as I passed. At first, I figured this was the natural instinct to watch a dead man walking, but this was not the case—some of my coworkers winked, others smiled and gave a thumbs-up, still others nodded in that sharp, professional manner that young executives must spend hours practicing in their mirrors at home.

Much about this, obviously, struck me as rather strange: (1) that I had seen the manager being led away in the traditional manner of dismissal, a dismissal of which I believed myself and my poor performance in Contracts to be the direct cause; (2) that, because I wanted to avoid scrutiny, I was usually among the first employees at my desk each morning—and had in fact come in even earlier than usual, owing to my night on the couch and my fitful otter dreams—but today everyone else was already there, as if they were waiting for me; (3) that they all seemed to know something I didn't, something about me; and (4) that just as I was about to enter my cubicle, out popped Smith with a sort of Al Jolson move, a ta-da move, arms out to the side in presentation of himself, weight on one leg, head cocked, vaudeville grin on his face, and he led the entire floor in a raucous rendition of "For He's a Jolly Good Fellow," which rendition would have been rather touching in its raucousness, had I even the slightest idea what I had done to merit it.

After the song, me still outside my cubicle, there was much backslapping and carrying on, many *Go get 'em, Tiger*s and *You're the man*s, even a *Well done, Perkins* from an old-schooler I couldn't identify in the melee. I thanked them all, because there seemed to be little else to do, and as I thanked them they slowly moved away, all but Smith, who stood there by my side the whole time, as if we were somehow in this—in what?—together.

I looked at him, and he made a motion with his hand, directing me into my cubicle, a motion that said, Well, let's go, and so I did. There was a box with all the things from my desk sitting on the floor by my chair and a bright orange Post-it note on my computer monitor. Written there in heavy black felt-tip ink were the words: *Perkins! See me! Schmelling!*

All those exclamation marks! And why was my stuff—four copies of *Newsweek*, three of *Time*, a half roll of Life Savers (Wint O Green), an unopened Cross pen and pencil set, a spare tie (always keep one in your desk, Dad had said, one of the last things he'd taught me before his heart exploded)—in that cardboard box on the floor? It could only mean one thing. But then, why were all the others so proud of me, winking and backslapping and congratulating me with song? Could it be that they all hated the IC, that they envied my imminent dismissal? And really, what had I done that was so outrageous? All I had done was not ask any questions; really, it was a matter of

respect for the IC and its decisional prowess; I had gone where
they told me to go, read what they told me to read, sort of, and
signed what they told me to sign, and if I had been doing such
a bad job, why had it taken six months for them to notice? I
had certainly not done anything like Terrence McNeil, nothing even as bizarre as what I'd watched this Schmelling do not
once, but twice, in successive weeks, what he had apparently
done enough times before to become a hero to everyone on
seven and God only knew what other floors as well. And now
he—Schmelling!—wanted to see me—Perkins! Perkins who had
never done anything truly wrong in his life, Perkins who just
wanted things to go easy, who didn't make waves, who kept his
head down and turned his work in on time, who had a house
and a wife at home—sure, she's a little odd, she's an artist, try
to understand—and if they wanted me to go back to PR, I'd
go. It was all a terrible mistake, but it wasn't *my* mistake, see,
and the thing is, I was only trying to keep whoever had made
the mistake from getting in trouble, I wanted to be a good team
member, and yes, I should have known better, I know Contracts
is far too important, Contracts is no place for a person like me,
Perkins! I'll never let it happen again. I promise.

At that moment, I heard a noise outside the cubicle. At first
I thought it was my heart again, but the sound soon grew too
loud even for that. It was a clap, then a stomp, then a clap, then
a stomp, and soon all the employees on the seventh floor were
doing it, clap, stomp, clap, stomp, in unison, and somewhere in
the midst of it all, a woman began to sing, the words, if there
were words, unintelligible, the tune a whiny, unmelodic descant
above the percussion of clap, stomp, clap, stomp. I looked out
and saw Smith standing across from me, sweat popping out of
his forehead and that forehead red again, much more so than
the day before. He was clapping and stomping and clapping
and stomping, and his teeth were clinched, his mouth a rictus of
pleasure and pain at once, his yellow teeth glowing against the
redness of his cheeks and neck, his eyes shut tight behind the

thick black frames as if he were so transported that to look on anything in a world as banal as this would be unholy, unnatural.

Afraid to move from my cubicle, I decided—*decided* is too strong a word, I was beyond deciding anything—to stay where I was and wait for whatever was causing this apocalypse to come to me. But I was beyond being able to do even that, beyond being able to do nothing. As if some unseen, giant, but still gentle hands had hold of me, I felt myself being led—not drawn, but led—out into the hallway between the cubicles. It was an irresistible force, and I didn't even try to avoid it. I knew that whatever I would see on the other side of my partition would change me forever, irrevocably, from being who I was to being someone I was not prepared to be, and I could only hope that somehow, as I had been led to Contracts and led to the window to watch Schmelling that first day, I would be led to an understanding of my new self, to adapt and grow and somehow live with what I would soon become.

There in the hallway, the workers were lined up, clapping and stomping, clapping and stomping. The woman singing was now in a wailing frenzy of sound, and there was no longer any question about words; it was just sound, animalistic, primal, going from groaning to screaming and haphazardly hitting every octave in between. Some people were falling on the floor and rolling about in some kind of corporate Pentecostalism, still clapping and stomping all along. The room, the floor, had become incredibly hot, from all the strenuous activity of the untested muscles and lungs, yes, but also from some other source, as if hell, if you believe in that sort of thing, had opened a branch office right here on seven. I was beginning to come back to myself in some way, to realize that what was happening here was wrong, and again, that urge to flee that I had felt briefly the day before returned to me.

I thought of the box of stuff on the floor near my desk, turned right to look for it, and there was Smith, grinning wildly. I turned my head left, and there was Smith again, still grinning.

I looked away, closed my eyes, and set my feet to run the gaunt-
let of my writhing coworkers, but just as I did, I felt Smith lean
in near my ear. "Are you ready for Schmelling?"

I opened my eyes, and I saw him.

It was Schmelling, and this time he was walking—if you
can call it that—under the weight of an enormous ledger that
he carried on his back. The book was as large as a queen-size
mattress, made of brown skin the color of cedar, its brass rings
as wide as Hula-Hoops, the pages thick and coarse as canvas
inside. I don't know how he was able to carry the thing by himself. I knew he was strong—you try the crabwalk sometime, it's
tough—but I would have thought ten men would have strained
under the weight of the astonishing book, and it hurt me to see
him bearing it alone. Forget for a moment that I should have
been thinking, What the hell is the deal with this huge ledger?
And why is he lugging it through this madhouse to begin with?
For all I can tell you is that at that particular moment, my only
thought was to help him with his burden.

So I did. I met him halfway across the room, and he, blue
eyes popping, face purple with stress, his sandy blond hair mat-
ted with sweat, looked up at me from beneath the ledger. All
noise in the building, save the sounds of our heavy breaths,
stopped immediately when our eyes met.

I said, "I'd like to help you with that, Mr. Schmelling."

He grunted something that was probably not a word, and
at first looked at me with demurral. But I wouldn't move, and
slowly he assented, and slowly he began to jog the ledger higher
on his back so I could get my shoulders underneath. I finally
did and discovered I was correct about the weight of the book.
Together we started to move, and the singing woman sang,
Aaaiiieeeeeeee! and the clapping and stomping started again, and
we carried the ledger together. I was immediately tired from
the strain, but I never even thought of putting it down, of not
carrying my share of the load. After a while, the tiredness disappeared, and it was as if we had somehow shuffled off the limits

of our selves, the limits that fatigue and fear and pain place on us in this life, and so we carried on, I never asking where we would stop, and he never telling.

Finally—I have no idea what time it was, it was late, it was dark outside the windows—we came to an area of the floor that was cleared of cubicle partitions, and there we set down the book.

Smith and a couple others scurried out to open the front cover, then they turned several pages at a time, looking for one that was blank. Two of the women rolled caster-bottomed office chairs beneath Schmelling and me, and we collapsed into them. I was too tired at that point to even look at the book, and so instead I simply slumped forward with my head in my hands. I really cannot tell you what I was thinking, other than I remember the incredible fatigue and the incredible sweetness of having that ledger lifted; I felt so light, so empty. It seems to me now that at that moment, all of my thoughts had been cleared away, that my mind was indeed a clean slate, tabula rasa, like a newborn child's, ready to be filled again with new thoughts, new ideas, new attitudes and visions, as if, from then on, everything would be new. I wasn't even sure I knew my name.

I felt a hand on the back of my neck, strong and sure, rubbing the soreness out, comforting, loving, and I knew it was Schmelling, and for a time, that was all I could think: Schmelling, Schmelling, Schmelling! All of my worries and regrets and doubts and fears, about my job, about my father, about Marcie, faded away. And I loved him, and I looked up into his face and I knew that he loved me. I put my arms around him, and we rolled our chairs together into a grasp, an embrace, a bond I knew would last as long as life, or at least until retirement age, or, who knows, maybe for all eternity.

LUBBOCK IS NOT A PLACE OF THE SPIRIT

I have thought on numerous occasions that the best thing to do about Clive is to kill him and then bury him out in the desert somewhere. Clive is problematic because he knows the following things that I wish he did not know:

1. Allison is not really my girlfriend.
2. I've been telling my family that Allison is my girlfriend.
3. I have a series of pencil drawings of Allison in various poses.
4. I have written a series of love songs to Jodie Foster.

Clive knows the last of these four things because one night I shared a small number of these songs with Clive, and he pretended to listen intently and honestly, only later to claim he would turn my songs over to the police. He knows about the third thing because when I'm out at class and he's sitting in the apartment supposedly writing a treatise about human consumption of natural resources, he instead spends his time going through my possessions. He knows about the second thing because one time I was on the phone talking to the man who claims to be my father—whose corpse is lately on my mind—and Clive heard me tell him that Allison is my girlfriend. He knows about the first thing because one time I was on the phone, pretending to talk to Allison, and Clive sneaked up on me and snatched the phone away and heard the dial tone. And then he sent me to the liquor store, because he is a bully of the intellectual and spiritual type, and he inspireth not.

ᵛ ᵛ ᵛ ᵛ

Clive says my brother called three times and where the hell have I been? He needs skim milk and a carton of Marlboros.

I have been to the following places:

1. English class, had the following experience after English class:
     Teacher: It's John, right?
     Me: It's John.
     Teacher: Where have you been?
2. The Golden Galleon, where I ate one-half of one-half of a Raiderburger with cheese. Left when I began imagining the hot globules of deep-fried fat pocking the pink skin of an infant.
3. The filling station.
4. The grounds outside Knapp Hall, where Allison lives.

Call your brother, says Clive.

This is the fourth day in a row that I have been unable to have a bowel movement.

ᵛ ᵛ ᵛ ᵛ

Clive says—Your brother called again today. Clive rarely leaves the apartment and never watches television, but today when I come home Clive is watching President Carter on television, talking about the economic crisis. Usually, when I want to watch television, Clive groans. Clive subscribes to at least fourteen different magazines, nine of which I pay for. I own a Gibson guitar.

ᵛ ᵛ ᵛ ᵛ

Song for Jodie #143 (a ballad)

I wouldn't have you on the streets, my little one———
I wouldn't have you out there on the streets
The nights I'd have you in between the sheets, my little one———
And rub the temples on your lovely head

⌄ ⌄ ⌄ ⌄

Today in English class the teacher taught a poem called "The Passionate Shepherd to His Love," by Christopher Marlowe. He also said that Christopher Marlowe was a spy who was killed in a tavern brawl. He also returned a test I did not take. I think Allison did well—she seemed pleased, and smiled a half smile, the bottom corner of one top tooth showing. *Fetching* is a word I'd like to use to describe it.

⌄ ⌄ ⌄ ⌄

Today I'm at home when my brother calls. Clive says—You get it, dammit. My brother says—How's school going have you talked to Mom and Dad lately how's Allison?

Look, I've got some work for you, my brother says.

I've got something I need you to do and you need something to do, he says.

A job would be good for you right now, I think, in a lot of ways, he says.

I'm running this guy's campaign for the House of Representatives, and I want you to come work for us, he says.

I just want to work long hours, I tell him.

No problem, he says.

⌄ ⌄ ⌄ ⌄

Clive distinctly remembers giving me a check for his half of the rent. Today I spent twenty minutes in the bathroom. I had the need to move my bowels, I felt the pressure, but when I sat down, nothing occurred. I strained. I stopped straining and rubbed my lower back, in the kidney regions, for quite some time, which is a technique. I tried straining while standing up to produce something, a beginning, some breach, some peeking of a head. After twenty minutes I managed to produce one small rock of feces, brown and cracked and cakey.

More than two hundred thousand Americans, mostly men, die on toilets every year.

⌄ ⌄ ⌄ ⌄

I want a job where I have to work long hours. I can't sleep nights. Allison was out tonight, with that little slut roommate of hers. They were out until nearly two in the morning.

⌄ ⌄ ⌄ ⌄

Song for Jodie #156 (a ballad)

Come live with me and be my love
Come live with me and be my love
Babe————————————————
Come live with me and be my love
Without you I can't seem to move
There's more in me than you can ever see from where you are
So come and live with me and be my love

⌄ ⌄ ⌄ ⌄

My brother sends me out armed with literature. Fliers and bumper stickers in a milk crate at my feet. The candidate's face on a sign. He grins. He has Lubbock on his mind. From Lubbock,

For Lubbock. I stand at the corner of Broadway and Tenth, near
Sneed Hall, holding my sign, armed with my literature that I
keep in a milk crate at my feet. If anyone comes up and asks
questions about the candidate, I'm supposed to be polite and
give them some literature. I'll work anytime, anywhere. The city's
motto is: Lubbock!

ˇ ˇ ˇ ˇ

Spoonbenders and other psychic phenomena. Christopher
Marlowe was a spy. Clive asks why haven't I paid the phone bill.
Clive says he distinctly remembers telling me to pick up some
paprika and Marlboros. Clive is writing a treatise on human consumption of natural resources. Clive knows about Allison.

Today I saw her leaving her biochemistry class. I was standing on the corner of Broadway and Tenth with my sign for the
candidate and my milk crate full of literature and bumper stickers. The following experience occurred:

A lady comes up to me at the corner. A lady who is probably
fifty years old, and dry. She asks me why she should vote for
the candidate. She's wearing pants. Black polyester pants tight
on her dry hips and flared out around her legs. And a white
shiny shirt with ruffles. What does he stand for? she says. In the
case of this experience occurring, I have been instructed by my
brother, director of campaign operations, to say the following
eight things:

1) The candidate believes in America first.
2) The candidate believes in lower taxes.
3) The candidate believes in God.
4) The candidate won't raise your taxes, like the
   other guy.
5) The candidate understands Lubbock.
6) The candidate puts Lubbock first.

7) The candidate thinks it's high time we took this
   country back.
8) The candidate asks for your vote for the House of
   Representatives.

Then I'm supposed to give her some of the literature I have in
my milk crate.

But when the Dry Lady asks me, I can't think of any of
these things. It's all in the flier, I say. I hold out a flier, but not a
bumper sticker. Bumper stickers are more expensive and should
only be given to those who specifically request them, number
one, and number two, my brother says, I'm supposed to get
some kind of feel for the people who specifically request bumper stickers, to try to gauge how firmly they support the candidate and how likely they are to actually go out on Election
Day and vote. He says there are lots of people who just want
to take a bumper sticker and then not do anything about it, not
even put it on their car. Why, I don't know, he says, but it's true.
People just like to get things of value, however small, as they're
walking around town. Especially college students. Which is why
we don't want to give out bumper stickers to just anyone and
everyone.

Here's what I think, the Dry Lady says. I think you don't
know *what* he stands for. I think he doesn't stand for anything. I
think if he stood for something you'd be able to tell me straight
out. I think you just lost my vote.

Just take the flier, ma'am, I say.

I don't want anything to do with your flier, and I don't want
you people knocking on my door anymore, either, she says.
I've had it with you. She either said that or How sad for you, I
couldn't tell which. She walked away, her dry legs bone-clatter-
ing up Tenth, and got into a gold Valiant parked there on the
street. I was sweating terribly.

So now I'm back on the corner with my sign, and Allison is
walking with her slut tramp whore roommate toward Bledsoe.

Her light blond hair shines even in the thin September twilight. Her friend is a toad of blood.

˅ ˅ ˅ ˅

Song for Jodie #161 (a ballad)

When you feel the terror of existence
I will comfort you like a child
When you feel awed by my insistence
Then I'll know your blood is running wild

When you mewl just like my little kitten
I'll know I have you
When you cry—————————————
When I leave—————————————
Then I'll know I have you

˅ ˅ ˅ ˅

Clive is drunk. He sends me out for more Evan Williams bourbon. He distinctly remembers writing me a check for his half of the rent. He remembers where he was sitting when he wrote the check. Among Clive's magazines:

- *The New Yorker*
- *The Nation*
- *Screw*
- *Southern Living*
- *Guns & Ammo*
- *Harper's*
- *Foreign Affairs*

Clive tells me that in twenty years the world will run out of carbon dioxide. I got the wrong size bottle of Evan Williams bourbon and now I have to go get more. My feet hurt from

standing on the corner all day with my sign. And because
I either erred or perhaps willfully disobeyed his instructions
and didn't get the right size bottle, I have to pay for the whole
thing.

Or else he'll call my parents and tell them the truth about
Allison.

⌄ ⌄ ⌄ ⌄

Today in English class the teacher talked about John Donne.
A poem called "The Flea." It's about how this girl should stop
holding out on him, since he's been bitten by a flea, and she's
been bitten by the exact same flea, and inside that flea their
blood is all mixed up, so why should she be so prissy about letting him have sex with her? Allison didn't seem impressed by
the argument. Allison does not exist in a world of blood and
fleas. The teacher returned another paper at the end of class.
Again, I didn't hand one in so I don't get one back. I knew this
one was due, but I was working, standing on the corner with my
milk crate, holding the sign for the candidate. Last week, when I
should have been working on my paper, I was holding my sign.
Anytime, anywhere.

All my life needed was a sense of somewhere to go. The
teacher has stopped asking why I haven't been coming to class.

⌄ ⌄ ⌄ ⌄

Clive.

Clive distinctly remembers giving me a check for his half of
the rent. Clive has no friends, no one ever visits Clive, no one
ever calls Clive, Clive never goes anywhere or sees anyone. Clive
refuses to let me look at any of his magazines, even though I pay
the subscriptions on more than half of them. Although sometimes when I'm in the bathroom, struggling with a movement,

he slides a dirty picture from *Screw* or *Leg Man* or *Oui* under the door. Have fun, Clive says.

˅   ˅   ˅   ˅

There was a rally for the candidate and my brother told me to come, first to hold my sign and act like I was just some person who came to the rally. Then he said, No, I have a better idea— you should come and pass out literature. Then the day of the rally he calls back and says, Listen, I've got a better idea.

He says, At the rally, the candidate is going to take questions from the audience. Except they're not really questions from the audience. Actually, my brother says, the candidate is only going to call on people from the campaign who are pretending to be people who just showed up to the rally. Do you get it? he says. Do you think you can handle it?

I tell him, All my life needed was a sense of somewhere to go.

Yeah, he says.

That night at the rally at the VFW hall, there are about thirty people there, and at least half of them work for the campaign. I recognize them from the headquarters, where I go every morning to get more fliers and bumper stickers for my milk crate.

The candidate is short. Shorter than he appears on the sign, which is just a picture of his head. But he looks taller on the sign.

The candidate says—I love Lubbock. I'm practically *from* Lubbock. I think Lubbock is God's country. Are you tired, he says, of the government getting your tax dollars? Are you tired of the liberals in Washington, DC, telling you how to live your life, and giving your money to deadbeats and dropouts? Some people clap, mostly the people from the campaign.

The candidate says—Do you want a congressman who believes in God? Isn't it time we started listening to what God is saying to our hearts, instead of what those liberals are saying to our heads?

Now I'll take some questions, the candidate says. I raise my
hand, but just as I do, I notice the Dry Lady in the crowd. The
candidate points his finger at me and says, Yes sir, you there.
Good to see the young people out tonight. You might could use
a haircut, but still, good to see you. He chuckles. Go ahead, sir,
you may ask your question.

The Dry Lady is looking at me. The candidate is looking at
me. My brother, who has been following the candidate around
the stage with the microphone cord in his hands, is looking at
me. I suddenly can't remember the question I was told to ask. I
suddenly panic.

I suddenly need to have a movement. I have gone to the clinic
at the university and have gotten literature that says that people
who have trouble with their bowels should never ignore the need
to have a movement, and should never resist the urge to go. It was
a pamphlet, which also listed a number of techniques.

The candidate and everyone else is still looking at me. The
candidate is still smiling, but I can see the smile changing. His
eyes are hardening, and his lower lip is coming up, flattening the
smile into something else. It feels like the candidate is standing
right on top of me, and now he doesn't seem short anymore.
I have to go.

I turn and run, the crowd parts, I'm waving my arms and
shouting. I don't know what to shout, so I shout, Lubbock!
Lubbock! At the door of the VFW hall are three people who
work for the campaign. I turn back toward the candidate and
my brother. I want to say something, I'm sorry, something. But
one of the people standing by the door grabs me and pushes me
out into the night.

I'm off balance now, but still running. Energy policy. Oil
drilling. That was what I was supposed to ask about. Clive says
the police would be very interested in looking at over 175 songs
about a fourteen-year-old girl, even if she is a world famous
actress and my chances of actually meeting her are—and you

have to understand this, he says—absolutely zero. I'm running to my car, trying desperately to clench my rectum, the movement is coming on its own now, and there's nothing to be done.

I stop between two cars, a Malibu and the gold Valiant that I know at once is the Dry Lady's car. I hurry my pants down and squat there in the parking lot.

I wait.

Nothing happens.

Allison. A long time goes by.

I strain. I push so hard I start to fall, and then when I try to stop myself from falling, my feet catch in my pant legs and I *do* fall, and when I fall the movement comes, hot and wet and smelling of metal, and it's on my legs and I'm trying to kick myself free from it. I can hear other people in the parking lot now, coming from the rally. I can see the Dry Lady in the lead. I crawl underneath her car, then crawl again underneath several other cars, until I get to mine.

I have a gun at home.

Clive does not know about the gun.

Clive does not know about the gun because I have concealed it very cleverly.

At the door of my car, I finally pull up my soiled pants, and then I drive to the filling station, where I buy two gallons of gas.

⌄ ⌄ ⌄ ⌄

When I get home, Clive says—Your brother called three times why haven't you paid the rent what's that smell?

⌄ ⌄ ⌄ ⌄

We all want different lives. Clive, my father, my brother. The candidate wants a different life. Even Allison. Why can't we have them? Why can't I give them to us?

I am more than I appear to be. I am waiting for the sun to shine. A long continuous chain, then suddenly, there is a change.

ˇ ˇ ˇ ˇ

Today on the corner the Dry Lady comes back again. She is wearing tan polyester pants of the same cut as before, and again the white shimmery ruffley shirt, and this time there is a red scarf around her hair.

I've opened my mind some to your candidate, she says. He's beginning to appeal to me. I saw him talk at the VFW hall the other night. He's young and dynamic. He says what he means and he means what he says. I believe in him. He's the kind of guy you'd like to have a beer with. I liked his answer about oil drilling, she says.

I say nothing.

I think your candidate has a bright future. I'd like one of those bumper stickers, please, she says.

I begin sweating again. It's late October and still eighty-five degrees in Lubbock. *Lubricious* is a word I'd like to use to describe it. Pistons churn. In Colorado, it's snowing.

I'll have one of those bumper stickers, please, the Dry Lady says now.

I've been standing here on this corner every day for eight, nine, ten, twelve hours a day for weeks. My studies are suffering. When people come by and ask me questions about the candidate, I give them fliers. Some people ask for bumper stickers and I give them to them. But the Dry Lady? No. I will not do it.

Here is a man who stood up.

ˇ ˇ ˇ ˇ

On the day after the rally at the VFW hall, when I went to pick up more fliers and bumper stickers for my milk crate, my brother called me into his office.

The candidate was in my brother's office with another man I didn't know.

What was *that* all about? the candidate says to me. Your brother said you were reliable. He said, we can put him to work. I said, why not, help the guy out, get him a little spending money, college student and all. I trust your brother. Your brother says, John's smart, he works hard. He just needs direction. I say to myself, that is one thing I've never had a problem with. Direction. I've always known where I'm going. But I know how to take advice, too. I know how to listen to the opinions of others, how to use those opinions to shape a consistence. Your brother says, Stick to taxes. Taxes, taxes, taxes. I trust him, but I like to give 'em a little Jesus, too. What do you think?

He's asking me.

I'm sorry, I say. I messed up. I really am interested in your energy policy, too, I say. My roommate and I have been having an interesting debate on this exact topic. It was the perfect question for me to ask you. In twenty years we're going to run out of carbon dioxide.

Exactly, the candidate says. Your brother said you were smart. I think you're weird. What do you think, Karl? he says to the other man, who stares at me without answering. Weird John, the candidate says. From now on that's your name. Weird John. Or how 'bout, Johnny Weird?

He stops for a moment, thinking. I can see him thinking. He's thinking about what to do to me. All I want is to get my literature and stand on the corner with my sign. The other man is still staring at me also.

Nope, the candidate says, finally, decisively. Weird John it is.

He stands up, and he and the other man move past me toward the door. Don't fuck up again, the other man says, his back to me. Then they are gone. My brother, who still hasn't said a word, sits in his chair, staring into his desk lamp.

˅ ˅ ˅ ˅

Give me one of those bumper stickers right now, young man, the Dry Lady says. Her scarf is a swirly red and purple paisley. She points at the bumper stickers in the milk crate on the ground near my left shoe. I move between the Dry Lady and the crate, nudge the crate backward with my heel. I still have not said a word.

What are you, some kind of idiot? the Dry Lady says. Are you nuts? Are you retarded? I'll have you know I am an extraordinarily influential Lubbock voter. And I'd say you just lost my vote. And I'm calling the campaign. I'll talk to the candidate himself about you. I can't believe that the nice young man I saw speaking the other night would have anything to do with you. I believe if he saw this he'd throw you in jail. That's where you belong. You fat jerk.

I still have not said a word. I have a gun at home, and from now on I'm bringing it to work. From now on, I'm bringing it everywhere. Lubbock is lubricious. Clive does not know about the gun.

Here is a man who stood up.

A small crowd begins to gather at the corner of Broadway and Tenth. Five or six people. Some of them I've seen before, walking around. We don't want to give bumper stickers to just anyone off the street. But today I give each member of the gathering crowd a bumper sticker—the couple of students who have wandered by, wondering what all the yelling is about, the guy who runs the sandwich shop across the street, the taxi driver, the old professor who shuffles by every weekday at this time, his briefcase scuffed and worn. I have to actually move out of the crowd to hand him a bumper sticker, and he looks confused at first and backs away, putting up his briefcase in front of his chest, and when I move toward him, the Dry Lady goes for my milk crate.

Here is a man who stood up.

I dive back into the small crowd and lunge for the milk crate. The Dry Lady's hand is nearly inside the crate, she nearly has her hand on a bumper sticker when I land on the crate, and her, and we're rolling out into Broadway. The Dry Lady is slapping at my head and my hands, and I'm trying to cover the crate and push her away and stand up all at once, and instead we both roll over again, farther into the street, and horns are honking, and the milk crate upends, spilling fliers and bumper stickers into the street, where all the people who have gathered, many more, most of them students, have now run into the street to grab the literature.

The Dry Lady is screaming and scratching at me. She scratches my face terribly, from just below my right eye all the way across my mouth and down onto my neck. Other people are grabbing at us now, hands on me, pulling, grabbing, kicking, several people.

When they finally pull us to our feet, the sleeve of the Dry Lady's shimmery shirt has been torn from her shoulder, her scarf is gone, and she's bleeding heavily from her mouth. My milk crate is still in my hand, but it's empty, and people are running everywhere with fliers and bumper stickers. There are two men yelling at me, and a man and woman are leaning in to talk to the Dry Lady, who is touching her hair with her hands and breathing quickly. My face hurts very badly and there's something wet in my shoes. But the Dry Lady does not have a bumper sticker, because here is a man who stood up.

You stay here with him, one of the men holding me says to the other one. I'm going to go get a cop. The other man holding me is very small, and when I turn to look at him it appears he has no interest in holding me. I pull my arm away from him, and he says—Wait a minute, buddy. But I don't wait. I walk back to the corner of Broadway and Tenth. We've rolled around for nearly half the block.

Across the street, on the campus green, a group has formed around a hipster guy in a striped pink shirt, who is holding my sign with the candidate's face and jumping up and down. The students all seem to have bumper stickers, and they're peeling them and sticking them on their shirtfronts.

Allison is at the edge of the crowd with her little slut room-mate, who is letting another hipster boy stick the bumper sticker to her rear end. Soon the hipster with the sign has formed his group into a parade, and he's off, leading the students in a happy march up the hill toward Bledsoe Hall. Allison looks back over her shoulder, once, for a brief second, and she recognizes me. She looks at me, and in that moment, for the first time in what has to be months, I smile. I know I'm smiling because it hurts my mouth where the Dry Lady scratched me. Allison is about to smile back, but just then that little bitch monster of a room-mate comes to her and pulls her away, and off they run, chasing the hipster with my sign and laughing. I watch them finally disappear over the hill.

Up the street, the man from before is coming back with a cop. I turn toward the campus, where some people are still mill-ing around, and looking away, I move quickly toward the English and Philosophy Building. I plan to ask my English teacher for asylum if I have to. I perform several acts of tactical evasion, including blending in with a crowd that has gathered to hear someone recite Shakespeare, and I cross from there into the cafe-teria, and back through Lowndes Hall to Eighth Street, where I've parked my car. I've escaped.

It is one week until Election Day. I don't believe that one should devote his life to morbid self-attention.

⌄ ⌄ ⌄ ⌄

Song for Jodie #186 (an urgent ballad)

When you smile at me
I know you're just a child
I know you're just a child
When you smile————————

⌄ ⌄ ⌄ ⌄

Clive says—The police called, your brother called, the landlord called, when are you going to pay the rent, have you seen my latest copy of *Field & Stream,* what happened to your face?

⌄ ⌄ ⌄ ⌄

It's 2:15 a.m. outside Knapp Hall. Allison is inside, her light is out. This is the third time I've walked around the dorm tonight. I can't sleep nights. I haven't had a solid bowel movement in over a week. I feel something is building here. This afternoon, fighting with the Dry Lady, I felt that if someone killed me, if a cop or somebody walked up and shot me dead on the streets of Lubbock, Texas, it wouldn't mean anything, that they wouldn't even file a report or give me a funeral.

I am not a person like other people.

After the fight with the Dry Lady, my brother said I couldn't stand on the corner anymore. He said the police had come to campaign headquarters looking for me. He said, Why can't you just do one thing right, John? He said he was being demoted.

This is the third time now the security guard has seen me pass the front doors of Knapp Hall. He comes outside and stands on the steps, looks at me. I keep moving toward the corner of the building. I keep looking up at Allison's window. I keep looking at the security guard, because I want him to. I really do. I want him to, just this once.

I have the gun tucked in my windbreaker. From now on, I carry it everywhere I go. It finally made sense to me after I killed Clive earlier tonight. The whole thing, for the past several weeks at least, has been planned by someone who means me harm.

I think a person ought to be like other people. I don't have that exactly right.

Anyway, I left Clive dead on the couch with four holes in his chest. Later, I will take him out into the desert and bury him.

Hey, buddy, the security guard says. The security guard is slim and wiry. I have always had great respect for the wiry.

Hey, he calls again, coming farther down the steps. What do you want around here, pal?

This is what I've wanted, what I want. So why do I keep walking? I suddenly think that maybe this wiry security guard has kids. That, even if it is a plan, and my brother and my father and Clive and the candidate and the hipster and Allison and her roommate and the Dry Lady are all involved, this guy's just a security guard who would be working here whether they ever launched their plan or not. At the very least, my studies have suffered irreparably, and you don't have the right to do that to other people. For any reason.

I keep walking, putting my head down. I only want to check one more time, to make one more circle round, then I'll go to my car, drive home, put Clive's body in the trunk, and take him out to the desert to bury him.

Now the security guard is coming toward me. I can hear him behind me, feel him reaching for me.

What's the problem, buddy?

I turn.

Jesus, he says, what happened to your face?

I point to Allison's dark window.

You see that bitch up there in that window?

He turns to look. I move my hand inside the pocket of my windbreaker and take it out. He looks back at me. He does not have a gun, but he sees that I have one, and he puts up his hands and begins to back away.

Take it easy, buddy, he says now, his palms facing me, shaking. I fire one shot just past his ear. Lights go on in Knapp Hall. The security guard falls to the ground and curls into a ball with his hands over his head. I fire one more shot at the front door. The bullet makes a tiny hole the size and shape of a nipple in the glass before continuing its trajectory through the building, unseen. More lights come on. The light in Allison's room comes on. I see her face in the window. I hear voices around me.

˅ ˅ ˅ ˅

It took three days to find a good spot to bury Clive. Texas is large. I was surprised at how I felt when I put Clive in the ground. I was touched by the look on his face and the sadness I experienced, which I think must be like the sadness other people might experience in a similar situation. After I buried him, I said a few words over his grave.

The night I buried him, I stayed in a motel in Plainview, where I had an exquisite and perfectly natural bowel movement. Almost a foot long, well-turned, smooth, colored in an appropriately normal way. It left no seepage afterward, and I felt so light I could fly. I thought at that moment—this is how people always feel.

˅ ˅ ˅ ˅

When I get back to the house the next day, Clive is there, reading a magazine, acting like I hadn't shot him and buried him in the desert at all.

The police have been here every day, Clive says. They say you are a fugitive from justice, he says. I showed them your songs about Jodie Foster. Tell you the truth, I'm pretty impressed by your emergence, Clive says, but they told me if I see you I'm supposed to call them right away. Also your brother has called over and over again. The landlord came by and said she was going to evict us if we didn't pay this month's and last month's rent by the end of the week, so I called your father.

Whose corpse is lately on my mind.

He sent me the money for the rent, Clive says. He wired it Western Union yesterday afternoon. He wanted to know what was going on with you. He wanted to know why you were acting so strange. He said the police had called him, too. I told him about the night you pooped your pants. I told him you got in a fight with an old lady. I told him I thought this was a very bad sign. I need you to drive me to the Piggly Wiggly to pick up the money.

Clive says this, who is dead and buried in the desert outside Plainview, Texas. For all the mysteries surrounding this case, I am almost positive of that one fact.

He wanted to know about Allison, Clive says.

What did you tell him, I say, reaching inside my windbreaker for the gun. I've already killed Clive once, I think, so what's the big deal?

I didn't tell him, John, Clive says. I think you have to tell him, Clive says. I think you're a pretty all right guy, you know, you're just having some problems with things. I don't think you like Lubbock very much, for one, and I don't blame you for that. And I don't think you like yourself, or your family. I think you need some help. But you've been a good roommate to me—you help me with my errands, and you don't watch too much television, and after you get out of jail and get your other problems sorted out, I'd be happy to have you for a roommate again, so long as you can talk your father into paying your half of the rent while you're away.

I take my hand away from the gun inside my windbreaker.

Thanks, Clive, I say.

He's coming here, Clive says.

My father?

Yes, he said he was going to drive out this morning. He'll be here tomorrow.

He's coming here?

Yeah, Clive says. You ought to get this place cleaned up. But first, take me to Piggly Wiggly. I'll wait a couple of hours before I call the police.

⌄ ⌄ ⌄ ⌄

This time I drove Clive well into New Mexico, dug another hole near Vaughn, and buried him again. We drove all night, me and Allison, with Clive dead in the trunk. Allison liked the mountains and the desert landscape. She said it reminded her of the hills in Ernest Hemingway's story "Hills Like White Elephants," which I know we were supposed to read for English class.

I didn't read it, I say.

No, she says. You wouldn't have.

When Allison and I get back to Lubbock, we make love in the front seat of my car in the dorm parking lot at Knapp Hall. She'd invite me in, she says, but after I took a shot at the security guard, it isn't safe for me around here. She kisses me deeply, holding my penis in her hand, then she scampers from the car and up the steps to her dorm.

I'm still watching her when she stops and comes back to the car.

Come and get me tomorrow, she says, and take me to vote. And after that we'll kill my roommate and you can move into the dorm with me.

⌄ ⌄ ⌄ ⌄

There's a rally that night for the candidate at the ballroom of the Lubbock Ramada Inn. I have the gun in my windbreaker. The crowd at the Ramada is a good bit bigger than the one at the VFW a few weeks ago, and I see some people I know, but more that I don't. I have on a green baseball cap I bought at a filling station in Roswell, New Mexico, where Allison and I stopped on our way back from burying Clive.

The candidate is standing on the stage in front of the ballroom. One more day, he says. I thank you for your support, he says, and I ask you for your vote. I see my brother in the crowd holding a sign just like mine. There is a man standing next to him who claims to be my father. On the other side of him is

Clive, whom I am frankly surprised to see, since I have killed him and buried him twice in two different states.

I can still smell Allison. Of all the things that have happened, I was gladdest to determine that she was not involved in the plot. Christopher Marlowe was a spy. I have my hand on the gun, and I'm moving toward them. I will shoot my brother once, my father three times, and the candidate twice. But in what order? I should probably shoot the candidate first. I will also have to shoot Clive again, even though this apparently doesn't do any good.

It's hard to believe how calm and happy I feel. But then, maybe it shouldn't surprise me. This is it. This is what my life has been moving toward. Pure force. And then, the end.

ˇ ˇ ˇ ˇ

Song for Jodie, #200 (a ballad—poss. title: The Last Song?)

You don't know me but
You'll never know me now
You'll never know how
Much I need you
How much I need you———————————————

ˇ ˇ ˇ ˇ

I am within ten yards of my brother and Clive and the man who claims to be my father. They have not seen me. The crowd seems to part from the force of my will. My hand is on the gun. I am going to kill them. And after that, my life will be different. I will never be a person like other people.

But when the candidate says, I'd be happy to answer some of your questions, I stop. I look to the stage. I am wearing a green baseball cap. I raise my hand. The candidate is looking directly at me.

You there, he says. The young fellow in the baseball cap. Nice to see the young people out here tonight, although my momma always told me to take my hat off indoors. He chuckles. I take off my hat.

The candidate is looking at me and smiling the smile from the sign. He is waiting. People are turning to look at me. My brother and Clive and the man who claims to be my father. They are all looking at me, one hand raised for the question, one hand still on the gun.

What do they see? Do they see a man who stood up? Do they see a person like other people? They're moving toward me now, not just my brother and Clive and the man who claims to be my father. The whole crowd, the candidate, Lubbock itself. The whole entire world, all those dead babies and those old men who died and all the women anyone ever loved and all the women who went unloved and the animals and the stars and the distant planets—it's all moving toward me, and I can feel myself in the center of it. I am no longer God's lonely man. I just need some help, some direction. I can be redeemed. I *can* have a different life.

I look back to the candidate, he is still smiling, still waiting patiently. He is looking at me as if he admires me, as if he knows that I *am* a person like other people. At that moment, whatever else the candidate may ever do in his life, he's heroic. He has saved not only his own life, but my brother's and Clive's and the man who claims to be my father's, and probably mine, and at this moment, I would do anything in the world for him. I realize that holding my sign in the heat and the dust and the rain and the sweat for six weeks, every day for eight, ten, twelve hours a day, that is nothing. That's the least any man should do for his candidate. You get a job, you become the job. If he could look into my soul and see the gun in my hand, and if he asked me to pull it out and kill, I would do it, without hesitation. If he sent me to war, I would go. I am his, and he is mine, and I will never forget the goodness he has done for me, and the goodness in his beautiful heart.

Go ahead and ask your question now, son, he says. I love him. My brother and Clive and the man who claims to be my father are here now. I am ready to ask my question.

We need to drill for more oil in this country, I say. I spent thirty minutes at the filling station tonight for two gallons of gas. It seems like your opponent doesn't care about people like me. He wants us to keep depending on Arabs for our oil, when we've got good American oil right here in Texas. My brother reaches me and puts his hand on my arm. The man who claims to be my father is on the other side now, and they're leading me, gently, away from the stage and toward the door. I look back up, one more time, to the candidate, who smiles and says, Thank you, I'm glad you asked that.

⌄ ⌄ ⌄ ⌄

It's three months after the election, and I'm in Colorado now, staying, for the time being, with the people who claim to be my parents. I have decided that there's very little virtue in not accepting them as such—what good would it do? These two people have actually been very nice to me, for most all of my life.

I've gotten letters from Lubbock. The prosecutor there has decided not to bring charges against me for assaulting the Dry Lady. When the police went to interview her, they found that the Dry Lady had turned her entire house into a shrine for the candidate. There were bumper stickers and posters and signs and hundreds of little candles lit all through the house. The DA told all of this to my father—she said she was trying to light a candle for every person who had voted for the candidate on Election Day. You could feel the heat from the front yard, and she was, the DA said, about a half-dozen votes away from burning the whole neighborhood down. He said she was actually employed by the campaign in some obscure way, that they were investigating her for vote fraud, and that bringing charges against me would only muddy the waters. He told my father that the Dry Lady was obviously unstable. I didn't bother to disagree, but I knew exactly how she felt.

My father wrote a large check for a scholarship to help campus security guards take evening classes at Texas Tech, and a smaller one to replace the front-door glass and some plaster at Knapp Hall.

Clive has also written, and his letter was very nice. Although he said he sold most of my things, he is keeping my Gibson guitar and my songs for Jodie, which were returned by the police. I'll just hang onto them for you, he said in his letter, and you can get them when you come back to school. Then, in a PS, he said—Maybe I'll just hold onto them for when you're famous someday. Ha-ha, Clive wrote.

Which is fine, because I won't ever be going back to Lubbock again. Dr. Croon at Clear Branch has agreed with my assessment that Lubbock is not a place of the spirit, and he's also pretty much convinced old nutso me that there's no sense in writing any more songs to Jodie, or to anyone else, for that matter. I don't really know how to play the guitar, for one thing.

I haven't heard from Allison, but Dr. Croon says I'm better off without her. Dr. Croon says hard work is its own reward, and he provided me with a job with the grounds department at Clear Branch and a prescription for stool softener, and more than anything, this has had a healthful effect on my day-to-day outlook. *Salutary* is a word I would like to use to describe it.

The other day I got a letter from the candidate!

I'd written him a while back, before I checked out of Clear Branch, and I told him how very sorry I was that he'd lost. If my terrible behavior cost you even one vote, I will not be able to forgive myself, I wrote him. I thank you from the bottom of my heart, I wrote him, for the kindness and the chance to serve on your campaign. It was, I told him, the proudest work I'd ever done in my life. I hope, I wrote, that I didn't let you down. The fear that I had failed him, I said, has been the one regret I had been unable to shake since coming to this place.

The other day I got his reply. Dr. Croon delivered it to me, his breath huffing in white puffs to the north parking lot, where I was shoveling snow. I opened the letter there and read two sentences, two sentences I've read again and again, for every nuance and intonation in them.

Cheer up, Weird John, the candidate wrote. *There's always another campaign.*

The Thing about Norfolk

The woman downstairs couldn't stand Tom and Patty's dog. This was in Norfolk, Virginia, where Tom had gone for graduate school, and they lived in a Cape Cod–style duplex on Graymont Avenue. Tom and Patty had the upstairs, the woman and her twelve-year-old son lived downstairs.

When Tom took out the dog in the mornings, the boy from downstairs would come out and pat the dog and chase it around for a moment. He was a nice boy with a cringingly thick hillbilly accent. He'd ask questions about the dog, what they fed him, what breed he was, how big he was when they first got him, questions that seemed to occur to the boy haphazardly. There was no father involved, and Tom felt sorry for the boy. Even if his mother was rude and the boy's questions were strange, Tom tried to be nice to him.

"I like this dog," the boy said one morning. "I always wanted me a dog."

"Maybe your mother would get you one," Tom said, "if you promised to take good care of it."

"Well, I don't think right now's the time to ask Momma 'bout a dog," the boy said. "And she sure don't like this one."

"Sorry," Tom said. "We're working on it."

The problem with the dog: Tom and Patty would admit, *did* admit, that the dog was not well trained. They often joked that they probably shouldn't have kids if they couldn't properly raise a dog. They'd tried obedience school, they'd put in the work, but the dog—part Border collie or part beagle, part boxer or

pit bull—the dog was a nervous dog, high-strung, constantly
on alert. There was no controlling it. The main problem was
the way the dog would launch himself down the stairs at the
first notice of sound or movement on the porch or in the front
yard. The stairs leading to Tom and Patty's floor of the house
ran down the west wall of the downstairs living room, and Tom
and Patty were sure, admittedly, that it was terribly disconcert-
ing to be watching television or reading a book or doing any
other normal living room–related things, thinking everything was
quiet and peaceful, and then a squirrel or a mailman or a gentle
breeze against a windowpane would transport the dog into a con-
niption of mad, yawping barks. You'd hear the dog tear across
the hardwood floors to the stairs, his toenails scratching vainly
for purchase before, likely as not, he'd go into this thumping
hip-slide—you could hear his legs wheeling, spinning—before he
would project himself down the ten or twelve stairs and land,
head against door, with a crash that sometimes, the woman
downstairs claimed in her notes, dislodged knickknacks from
the shelves, and sometimes, she claimed, loosened pictures from
the walls.

Is there anything you can do about your dog? the first note read.

The dog was up and down the stairs a dozen times tonight, another
note read, one night when Tom and Patty had gone to a movie.
You have no idea how aggravating it is.

Don't you care about being good neighbors? another note read. *We
don't make noise, we lived here for three years and we never had trouble like
this. I'm calling Mr. Hoard.*

Also, the duplex was haunted. When Tom visited Norfolk
and picked out the duplex, he took a number of photographs to
bring back to St. Louis to show Patty. There's one he took from
the sidewalk, focused on the lovely second-floor sunporch that
fronted the house, and there in the corner window, obscured by
the sun, is a ghosty, featureless little boy in some sort of gauzy
garment, like an old-fashioned sleeping gown, his hand raised

as if waving, or as if he's about to put it to his brow to shield his eyes from the sun. What was strangest about the photograph was that Tom and Patty didn't notice the boy in the photo until after they'd moved in. They were putting together some pictures of the place to send to her parents, and there was the little boy.

"It sure looks like a little boy," Tom said.

"It *is* weird," Patty agreed.

Tom called the landlord, a polite if efficiently businesslike fellow named Mr. Hoard, and asked him if anyone had ever told him about seeing ghosts in the duplex. Mr. Hoard told Tom that there were stories. The house had been built in 1917, along with all the other ones on the street, to billet doctors working at the naval hospital during World War I. A doctor in one of the houses, apparently unable to mentally compartmentalize the carnage he witnessed at work, went crazy and killed his whole family with his service revolver. But Mr. Hoard said no one was sure which house the murders had occurred in, and anyway, he had never had any tenants report any problems. He then told Tom that the neighbors had complained about the dog again. "We're working on it," Tom said.

Strange things did happen—for example, Tom and Patty would frequently find that plugs had been unplugged during the night. You'd go into the kitchen in the morning and the coffeemaker was unplugged. You'd turn on the TV and have to get up to plug it in. Once, Patty looked for weeks for a favorite pair of shoes before finding them sitting on the front porch, where she had definitely not left them. One time the milk disappeared from the refrigerator.

It was a full gallon, they'd bought it at the store only the day before. When it was obviously not in the fridge, Tom and Patty searched. They checked the car to see if they'd forgotten it in the trunk. It was not left on the porch or steps. They searched every room, thinking they'd distractedly set it down somewhere. But Patty clearly remembered putting it in the fridge.

"I moved those olives and the orange juice and I put it right there," she said. There was a milk-gallon-shaped space on the refrigerator shelf.

"It *is* weird," Tom said.

"It is *really* weird," Patty said.

Also, there was the family next door. Like the woman downstairs—who did some sort of work on the base—and like most people in Norfolk, the people next door were Navy people. The husband was an officer who'd leave every morning in his uniform. They had a daughter, fifteen or sixteen, who consistently, constantly, repeatedly showered with the blinds open in the bathroom whose window faced the eastern side of Tom and Patty's duplex. From Tom and Patty's kitchen window, they could get a teenage nudie show nearly every night. She would undress and get in the shower and get out and dry off, all with the window open. But some nights she would use the window itself as a kind of full-length mirror, checking out her various parts and angles. One night, about ten days after they moved in, the girl kept looking at herself in the window over her shoulder, reaching back and flicking the cheeks of her ass, checking its tautness. Fifteen minutes this went on.

"Old Hoard should market this," Tom said. "Forget selling people on the sunporch and the cozy backyard."

"You should stop looking," Patty said.

"I've got a fifteen-year-old ass in my face while I'm doing the dishes," Tom said. "You want me to stop looking how?"

"I don't know," Patty said.

"You want me to call a plumber, move the sink to the other side of the room?" Tom said. "You want me to go over there and have a stern talk with her?"

Because this was the thing about Norfolk—the way everyone kept to themselves, or the way they kept away from the non-Navy people like Tom and Patty. Tom and Patty loved the neighborhood—old trees and old houses and canals and history just blocks from their front door. There was an old church with a British cannonball lodged in its seaward wall. After growing up in St. Louis, they loved being so near the ocean. There were wild, squawking parrots that roosted in a catalpa tree just a few houses down, there were good seafood restaurants, and Virginia Beach was a half-hour drive. In the mornings, you could smell the sea. It should have been a great place to live, but the grad school wasn't so hot, and Patty was social, and liked people and getting to know people, but everyone in Norfolk ignored them, which made her hate the place. On nights when they should have been out, Patty spent most of the time on her phone, or on Facebook, talking to friends from home about how much she hated Norfolk.

"Everyone treats me like I'm some sort of child," she said one night. "I'm twenty-six years old. I have two college degrees."

"Is it possible," she said one Saturday after a trip to the store, "that this has been genetically ingrained in these people somehow? Loose lips sink ships?"

"You should have seen me, Tom," she said one morning after walking the dog. "This random woman comes up, she looks like a normal fiftyish woman, and I say *good morning* and I say *I'm sorry about the dog jumping up*, and I can tell the whole way she's not going to respond. I say *nice weather* and I say *getting cooler* and the next thing you know I'm following this woman up the block, screaming at her, *Good morning! Good morning!* She actually put her hands over her ears and ran away."

The next-door neighbors, for example, hadn't said a dozen words to either of them as the weeks went by that they'd lived there, so it wasn't like Tom or Patty could go next door and . . . how would they even *approach* such a subject? Hi, Commander, Mrs. Waller, how are you? We're your new next-door neighbors. We brought over a Bundt cake, and do you know for the last month we've been watching your daughter naked through her bathroom window? It was sad even for Tom, who really didn't know until he moved to Norfolk that he did need friends. He'd always had his books and his work, but even in his program at

school he'd made no friends—it was sad, but true, that the nic-
est anyone in Norfolk had been to him was the boy downstairs,
who more and more was out front in the mornings, waiting for
Tom to come down with the dog.

"There's old pup pup," the boy would say every morning.

"There he is," Tom would say, and the two of them would
have an amiable conversation like any two other men in America,
except that one of the men was twelve and kept asking peculiar
questions about the dog. Tom wondered if maybe the boy had
one of those autisms that render you incapable of normal social
interaction.

How do you cut his toenails, the boy would ask. Have you
ever tried one of those vacuum brushes they do on the TV?
What kind of treats does he like? How high can he jump? *Haw
hi kinnee jump?* And when Tom would answer, the boy's response
would be a sound it is very hard to replicate in words, a kind
of appraising *hmmm* sound, but one that also sounded sort of
sarcastic, like the boy was not appraising the dog but appraising Tom, and finding him, or his answers, wanting. But Tom
was also nervous during these morning conversations that the
mother would come out and confront him face-to-face about
the dog, which, in all the time of leaving notes, she had never
done. How often do his ears need cleaning? Did you ever think
about bobbing his tail? Has he ever bit anybody? It was almost
like the boy thought about nothing but the dog all day long,
formulating a new list of questions for the next time he and
Tom would meet. Sad, but no one else in Norfolk put this kind
of energy into talking to Tom.

Then there was this: One night, during an especially intense
bathroom show, Patty dropped to her knees in front of Tom
and sucked him while he watched the child across the way. Just
as Tom was about to come, the girl flipped off the lights and left
the bathroom, and Patty, as if on cue, rose to her feet and took
Tom's hand between her legs. "I'm so wet I can't even walk,"

Patty said, and Tom raised her skirt and fucked her there against the kitchen counter while the dog watched from the doorway.

Almost immediately after what was unquestionably the single greatest sexual experience of their three years together, Patty felt incredibly guilty. They sat on the bed and Patty cried. Tom tried to console her, but failed.

"We won't do it again."

"But we did it."

"What's the big deal? It's just a little kinky. It's not like we're child pornographers or something."

"What *are* we like?" Patty said.

"It's not like the girl is eight or something."

"It's not like anything, huh? Then why did you get so hot?"

"Because *you* were hot, Patty."

"Yeah, I'm real hot compared to that."

"Listen, Patty," Tom said. "I didn't ask you to go down on me in the kitchen."

"Yeah, but your dick was already hard when I pulled it out," she said. "You've never fucked me that hard. You've never—"

"Patty," Tom said. "Calm down, okay? Let's just go to sleep."

Two nights later, it happened again, exactly as before. And then:

"You want kinky. I don't mind kinky, Tom. I'll dress up. You can tie me to the bed if you want. You can spank me. You can have my ass."

"I don't need all that," Tom said.

Weeks passed. It happened again and again.

"Then why is the only time we have sex anymore after we watch her in the window?"

"That's not the only time we have sex."

"Oh yes it is," Patty said.

"Well, hell, she's there every night."

"Not every night."

"Anyway, Patty, most nights. And I am, I will remind you,

a man, and that is a teenaged girl who right here in this state would have been a very marriageable person only a couple of decades ago."

"You prick."

"Why am *I* a prick?"

"You're a prick because all you think about all day long is getting through dinner and getting to those dishes. Our dishes have never *been* so clean. I couldn't *pay* you to help with the dishes before."

So now the question becomes, did they eventually stop? They did not. Nearly every time they did the dishes, they wound up savaging each other in the kitchen. There were different instigations, different positions. There was the thing with the spatula. One night, bent over a rolling microwave cart, she did give him her ass, demanded he take her ass. Tom decided it wasn't for him. At times food would intervene—vegetables, jellies, spices, sandwich meat. Patty became skilled at the sexual applications of various kitchen soaps. Some nights Tom didn't even want to that much. But they did it, and afterward there would be the same recriminations, the same guilt.

"Do you think this might mean I'm a lesbian?" she cried one night.

"I'm *worse* than a lesbian," she cried one night. "I'm a lesbian pedophile. Do they even *have* those?"

"I just wanted a normal sex life," she cried one night. "You've got me so fucked up now I don't even know who I am."

"Prison," she cried one night. "I can tell you right now, that's where this is heading."

One night she cried, "I'm going crazy."

And on top of all of this, the thing with the dog got worse and worse. They installed a gate at the top of the stairs, but the dog leaped over it or busted through it. They tried crating the dog when they left the house, but by now they hardly ever left the house, and you can't keep a dog crated all the time—it was cruel, and what was the point of having a dog in a crate? Tom installed an indoor invisible fence at the top of the stairs. Made things worse—the dog ran right through it and thrashed down the stairs even louder, yelping from the pain where the collar was zizzing him on the neck. Also, the ghost kept unplugging it. The notes from downstairs kept coming, kept getting meaner and meaner. Profanities, and so on. Old Hoard kept calling, demanding that they come up with a solution. The term *eviction* was actually employed. School wasn't going well for Tom. Patty had gotten a job in the registrar's office at the college, and she hated it there, too. They began to make plans to leave Norfolk. Old Hoard would keep their deposit for breaking their lease, but it didn't matter. Tom would finish out the semester, they would go back to St. Louis and apply to other graduate schools for next fall. Patty's father owned a PR firm, specializing in hospital accounts, and Tom could freelance there, and Patty could get her sub job back at the high school. And then one night, Tom had Patty bent over the kitchen sink where they could both see the girl, when they heard something hit the window.

They froze. Across the way, the girl had one leg hiked up on a laundry basket, applying lotion to her right inner thigh. When something else hit their window, Tom and Patty noticed the lights in the kitchen were on. How had they forgotten to turn them off? They always turned them off. They still hadn't moved—Tom's hands were on Patty's hips, and his penis was retracting from her of its own accord. Patty finally shoved him backward and crawled away. Tom focused on his own face in the window and on holding very still. For some reason, this seemed important, seemed all that was important. If you don't move, his face seemed to say to him, nothing else will happen. Time will stop. And then the light in the kitchen went out, and Tom couldn't see his face anymore.

Tom still didn't move, but now he could see down into the gravel driveway between the two houses. He lowered his eyes, and there, standing poised to toss another pebble, was the boy from downstairs. When he saw Tom look down at him, the boy set the pebble on the ground. The boy looked at Tom in his window, then looked at the girl in hers. Then he looked back at Tom and slowly wagged his finger, a terrible grin on his face. Then he ran back inside. Tom still didn't move. When he finally raised his eyes from the driveway, the girl's bathroom light was out. Something wet from his penis hit the top of his bare foot with a splat.

Tom finally turned from the kitchen sink. The house was completely dark. The dog was lying near the top of the stairs, waiting to charge when the cops arrived. Tom called for Patty and got no response. He looked in the living room, he looked in the bedroom. While there, he put on his pajama pants and a T-shirt. He looked in the bathroom, its shades drawn against the streetlight outside.

He finally found her on the sunporch, curled up in the corner below the window where they'd seen the ghost in the photograph. She was crying, quietly but fervently, and this time, Tom didn't blame her.

"Prison," she cried. "I told you."

"Patty, I've got to ask you," Tom said, sitting down cross-legged next to her. "How did you forget to turn out the lights?"

"I *did* turn out the lights," she said. "I *always* turn out the lights."

"But tonight they were on, and tonight's the night we got caught."

"I turned off the lights," she said. She started hitting her knee with a balled-up fist. She hadn't put any clothes on.

"Patty, the lights were on."

"I had my eyes closed," Patty said. "I was with *you*, not with her. I was fucking *you*, not fucking her."

"Wait," Tom said. "The lights *were* out."

"When I'm about to have sex in a window in front of a naked fifteen-year-old girl, I always turn out the lights," Patty said. "That's what I'll tell the judge."

"The lights *were* out," Tom repeated.

"She might be fourteen," Patty said. "Hell, she could be *twelve*—what do we know? We probably should have looked into that before we started this life."

"No, Patty, listen to me. The lights were out. I remember. Something happened."

"You've got to be kidding me," Patty said, finally turning to look at Tom, her mouth hanging open. "The ghost?" She'd cried so much the tips of her hair were wet, where they'd fallen in her face. "That's what you're going with, the fucking *ghost*? Good luck with that one. I'm pleading insanity. Women's issues. Hormonal imbalance. Hysteria. I'm not too proud, obviously."

She was right, of course—it'd been one thing to joke about living in a haunted house. It'd been one thing to write home or regale their Facebook friends with tales about the unplugged plugs and the missing shoes and the milk. It'd been one thing to blame the ghost for the way the dog behaved. It'd even been one thing to call out to the ghost sometimes, to talk to him like he was really there. But the ghost certainly had not turned on the kitchen light. Patty had simply forgotten it, and they'd both been too far gone in their game to notice it. Would *that* be a better defense? It's just a game, Your Honor. No one's hurt by it. The girl never even knew we were watching her. It had to be better than *the ghost turned on the lights.*

But wasn't this better still? Your Honor, we're terribly sorry the boy saw us doing that in the window. We're still newlyweds, we get carried away sometimes. It'll never happen again. The girl? What girl? I don't know what you're talking about. You say she was showering in that window across from our kitchen? I can assure you, sir, that we never saw anything like that—if we had, we would have immediately gone over there and told her parents. What kind of people do you think we are? I'm a graduate student, for crying out loud, not some kind of sicko. I'm offended, frankly. The whole accusation is absurd. I don't care what a twelve-year-old boy thought he saw, Your Honor. If the boy, the twelve-year-old boy, knows something about a naked teenaged girl in a bathroom window, maybe that's something you should ask *him* about.

Yes, that was better, but would Patty hold up? She was still punching a bruise into the top of her knee, crying like she really was hysterical. Now she stopped punching and began gripping her forearms, twisting the skin there like an Indian burn. What was this? Manufacturing evidence against him? Your Honor, look at my wounds.

"Patty, you need to get dressed," Tom said. "I'm sure the cops will be here soon."

"Oogie, boogie, boogie, boogie, blah, blah, blah," she said, knocking Tom's hand away where he'd reached out to her, her fingers twitching wildly in the air. "I don't want to talk to you anymore. I don't want to hear you talk. I have the right to remain silent."

"Patty, is this how you want them to find you, to find us?"

"That's exactly right, Tom," Patty said. "They've found us. They've discovered us. I never wanted to come to this town in the first place. You *had* to go to graduate school. Why did you have to go to the only school that let you in? Shouldn't that have been a sign?"

"Patty—"

"No," she said. "It should have been a sign to *me*. That's it. I should have seen this all along. My God, what am I going to tell my father? I was a teacher, Tom. A high-school teacher. I *taught* that girl. She was in every class I taught, and somewhere inside me, just waiting for you to get it out, was *this* person, this *thing*." She started pounding her knee again. "It's every man for himself now, baby. I'm going with he drove me to it. I'm going with he forced me. I'm going with insanity."

And after a while of all this, after a long while, they began to realize that the dog had not started barking, that no one had pulled up outside the house, no cops had come, no knocks on the door. It was incredibly quiet. For hours Tom and Patty sat there on the sunporch, until even they went quiet. At some point

Patty fell asleep, and Tom covered her with an afghan. Maybe Tom fell asleep. The next thing they knew it was dawn, and they might not have even noticed that if the dog had not risen from the top of the stairs and come to the sunporch, his cold nose nudging Tom to go out.

Tom and Patty looked at each other, then gathered the dog between them. The dog was warm and Tom and Patty were very cold. As they hugged the dog, Patty spoke.

"Tom," she said. "I want you to take the dog out and then come back inside. Then we're going to pack whatever we can fit in the car and we're leaving. The next time I walk out of this house, I want it to be to get in the car and for you to drive me home. I want to go home."

"Okay," Tom said.

"I don't care about the furniture, any of it," she said. "They can have it all. I just want to go home."

"Okay," Tom said. He stood up, stiffly, and the dog started hopping around the sunporch. "Come on," he said to the dog. He went to the stairs and put the dog's choke collar on, and slowly, quietly, they moved toward the front door.

It was a fine morning in mid-November. The grass in the front yard was heavy with dew. The parrots squawked in the catalpa tree. Tom and Patty's car was parked at the curb in front of the house. Moving out what they cared about could be accomplished in as little as an hour. The dog pulled him down the steps to the walk, and then to the sidewalk and on down Graymont. Almost immediately the dog peed and pooped, and Tom wrestled the dog back to the house. As they walked up the porch steps, a voice said, "I always wanted me a dog."

It was the boy from downstairs. He sat on the porch, his legs out, his back against the house, wearing the same clothes he had on the night before. Tom remembered his terrible wagging finger, his terrible grin. Tom said nothing, kept walking toward his door.

"So what, you gonna act like I'm not even here, like I'm not even talking to you?" the boy said. "How come everybody that moves into that upstairs apartment is so rude?"

Tom stopped. The dog kept jumping around, tugging at its leash, pulling Tom's arm. "Sit," the boy said. The dog sat.

"Lay down," the boy said. The dog lay down.

"He's a good dog," the boy said. "I always told Momma that he was."

"We're leaving," Tom told the boy.

"Everybody leaves," the boy said.

The boy looked up at Tom again, closing one eye against the brightness of the morning. He studied Tom for a moment, then laughed.

"Sheee-it," the boy said, and spat down into the holly bush at the front of the porch. "You think I'm gone say anything 'bout *that*? Man, I been watching that girl ever since we moved down from Staunton. That's the birthplace of President Woodrow Wilson."

The dog whined a bit but lay still on the porch.

"C'mere, pup pup," the boy said. He put his hand out and made a kissing sound. The dog crawled over, belly never leaving the porch.

"I ain't giving that up unless I have to," the boy said. He held both the dog's ears between his thumb and forefinger, rubbed them together. "I got the whole setup. Here in about a year or so I'm plannin' to go over there one day and put it in her, once I get a little bit bigger. You think she don't know y'all are watching her?"

"She knows?"

"Course she knows. She told me about it." The boy dropped the dog's ears and looked up at Tom. "Listen," he said. "Just how stupid a motherfucker are you?"

Tom said nothing. He couldn't. He was, for the first time in his life, truly considering the question.

"College, huh," the boy said, petting the dog under his chin.

"If y'all're leaving, I'll hang on to this dog. He's a good dog. I'll train him up."

Tom watched the dog and the boy. What choice did he have? And what difference would it make? He was sick of the dog, sick of this place. Dog and place and boy and girl and the woman downstairs and the commander and Old Hoard and the ghost and the parrots and the crappy school that had been the only one to admit him—they all deserved each other. It was really a favor, Tom thought, for the boy to take the dog and let them go on their way. And then, for just a second, he thought he had something clear in his mind.

"It was you," Tom said. "You're the one in the picture. You broke into our house and unplugged the plugs. You turned on the lights."

"What're you talkin' about?" the boy said, grinning that terrible grin from the night before. "Did you sleep at all last night? Look at you."

"How many people have you run out of here just like that?" Tom said. He kneeled down to be at eye level with the boy, who looked down at the dog. "Come on, kid—you got me, just tell me the truth. It was you. You got a key somehow or you found some way to get in. The whole thing was you."

"You're wiggy, man," the boy said. "I was just takin' out the trash when I saw you and your old lady. Scarred me for life."

"It was you."

"I don't know what you're talking about," the boy said, looking up, his face blank. "Now, I think y'all were saying y'all are gone go. You want some help loading up your shit?"

"No, thank you," Tom said. He couldn't be sure. And even if he was sure, what did that mean? Maybe it meant he wasn't *that* stupid a motherfucker, but what good did it do him?

"All right, then." The boy stood up and unleashed the dog, who sat next to him, perfectly still. "What's his name again?" the boy said, handing Tom the leash.

Tom told him. The word barely came out.

"What the hell kinda name is that?" the boy said. "Come on, pup pup, let's take us a walk, figure out your fuckin' name."

And the boy and the dog walked off north on Graymont. The boy started whistling a tune, high and sweet and clear. The wind was in off the coast, and Tom could still hear him whistling as they rounded the corner and disappeared into the dewy morning sunlight behind the Episcopal church on Trent.

MAYFLIES

The mayflies are spawning this time of year, in waves off the Coosa River. There must be a million of them pressed flat against the glass walls. It's pretty gruesome to look at, but all the places that stay lit up at night have them. They only live a few hours, then they fly from the river and fling themselves into the glass and die.

I've seen thirty-seven summers in this little town, thirty-seven years of mayflies. Women in my family live a long time. I'll see many more.

Sandy tells me they only live to give other animals, fish and birds and bats, something to eat, says she learned that in biology. A flying crop, her teacher called them. Sandy's marrying the ketchup bottles. She lays two or three towels out on one of the tables, then she sets the less full bottles on top of the more full bottles and seals them together with the ketchup gunk around the lips. She always makes a big production out of it, and it slows us down, but I've quit trying to tell her that. By the time she gets that done I've pretty much finished up all the side work, and Royce is no help either.

Royce hides out in the back instead of getting out the mop and cleaning all those mayflies off the walls. He's either in the mirror looking at his arm muscles, or he's sitting and smoking cigarettes and moping around and grousing about having to do even the simplest thing. No one makes him work here. *No one put a gun to your head.* That's what Bing says. He's the owner. Bing always says that. I hear it coming every time. A customer gripes about something—*Hey, no one put a gun to your head.* When the day girl complains about working a heavy lunch by herself—*Hey, no one put a gun to your head.* Bing wants to move to South Carolina and run a fishing rig, but he keeps coming back to the café. *Hey, no one put a gun to my head.*

I've got mustard stains on the cuticle of my right thumb. Ketchup, steak sauce, egg yolk all come out easy. But not mustard, no matter how I scrub. Royce is standing in the bathroom doorway with that chipped-tooth grin.

"I'm gonna go, Ms. Willet," Royce says. "It's about that time."

"You get those flies?" I say. There's a big male thumbprint on the women's bathroom mirror. I wet a brown paper towel and go to wiping on it, because I don't want to look at Royce, who thinks he's menacing me.

"No, ma'am, but there'll just be more tonight. I'll get 'em first thing."

When you'll be late, and Bing will have done it himself by then. Oh well, you know what Bing would say.

"Something on your mind, Ms. Willet?" Royce says now, in a little voice like you'd talk to a small child. I can see him in the mirror now since he's moved in behind me in the little bathroom. He smells like chicken grease and cheap cigarettes, and I know what's coming next. I'm back bent over the sink, working on my thumb, when Royce reaches up and puts his hand on my breast. I don't move it, or stand up. He presses himself up against me now, and I stand, and his other hand comes to my other breast. I let him go on a minute. It's my fault, and no one else ever wants to touch them. But it's not happening again. Not tonight.

"Go on, Royce," I say after a minute. "Get on about your business."

"I'm about my business now," he growls, trying to act all manly and evil and seductive. But he doesn't fool me. I know evil.

Four years ago my oldest boy, Ronnie, shot and killed my baby, Ford, with their father's .38. It was ruled an accident.

Ronnie's nineteen now, somewhere in Iraq with the US Marine Corps. Ford will always be nine. That is evil.

I knock his hands away and move past him out the bathroom door. Sandy's putting the caps on the last of the ketchup bottles. Royce doesn't follow me. I hear him hoot as the back door slams. Then his car starts up, and you can hear that all over town—a 1975 Dodge Charger he rebuilt from the tires up, the only thing Royce has ever worked at in his life. He makes his usual pass through the gravel parking lot, raising dust and spinning out, gunning his engine. It makes the walls shake, but no mayflies fall off. Finally, he pulls out of his spin and hits the paved road, his back wheels catching and straightening as he speeds away.

"What. A. Redneck," Sandy says. I want to tell her she's wrong, that Royce is not a redneck. Rednecks are called rednecks because their necks are red from working in the sun all day, and Royce wouldn't know work if it knocked him for a loop. He's a twenty-four-year-old child already well past the apex of his powers, I want to say. He's trash, and his people are trash, and his momma was definitely trash, because I went to high school with that one, but she's dead now, and so I say nothing.

"You about ready?" I say. There are still things to do, but I really will do them tomorrow—I'm covering for the day girl for the third time this month, not that I'm counting.

"Well, yeah, I'm ready," Sandy says, glad to be leaving early on a Friday night. I check the front door, then turn out all the lights as we leave through the back. There, more mayflies, in the primes of their lives, twitter and flash in the pool cast by the security light. We step quickly into the dark parking lot, but Sandy doesn't move fast enough and gets one stuck in her hair.

"Gross! Gross!" she says, swatting at it and then putting her book bag over her head as she trots toward my car. Sandy's mother drops her off in the afternoons and I give her a ride home most nights. She's on my way.

"I've never seen so many," she says, pulling the car door shut. "Aren't there more this year?"

"I don't know," I say. "Seems about like usual."

"They live for three years underwater. That's the larval stage."

We drive out along Rainbow Drive, what passes in Pine City for a main drag, and Sandy stares out the windshield at the waves of clear silver sweeping across the road.

"Then they come up out of the water," she says. "Do you know they can't eat when they come up?"

"I didn't know that."

"They only come up to mate," Sandy says, then pauses, then sighs. She's a melodramatic girl who claims to have big dreams. Her senior year's coming up at County. She's set to be valedictorian. Says next it's down to Auburn for vet school. So far she hasn't let any of these boys drag her down too bad. I've worked with Sandy for two years, but I don't really know her—I don't want to. Not that she's not agreeable enough, as these little Pine City princesses go. I'm just out of the getting-to-know-people business.

"And then, after they mate, they die," Sandy says now. "The males die right away. But the females have to go around and lay the eggs. Those are all females on the windows, all females flying around."

She looks in the mirror on the back of the visor and gently pulls strands of her brown bangs down over her forehead. I'll drop her at her house, she'll go in and change, and then she'll be on the phone for a ride to Hardee's. The high-school kids, and the ones who didn't leave after high school, they all hang out in the parking lot there. It's what Pine City has instead of a singles bar.

When I was Sandy's age it was Runt's, downtown. Runt-burgers for a buck, cheese and tomato twenty cents extra. Buck Willet with shiny black hair, chain-smoking Camel straights with his boot on the fender of his father's Le Sabre. Pabst Blue Ribbon from across the county line in wax soda cups. My sweaty back against green vinyl and the smell of his father's pipe mixing with Buck's Aqua Velva as he moved above me in the dimness from the streetlight at the corner of Cherry Street and Park. Then we'd go back to Runt's for more beer, and Buck would prop me there on the hood of his old man's car, like a fancy hood ornament or a trophy fish. I doubt that Buck Willet has ever in his life been more at home than he was in the parking lot of Runt's at eighteen years old. I got pregnant and married him. What does that say about me?

I'm not paying attention and almost miss the turn to Sandy's house. When she says, "Here it is," it makes me jump a bit in my seat and put the brakes on a little too hard. I've been zoning out like this more and more lately. Royce drives ninety miles an hour down residential streets. I never exceed the speed limit, but I'll be the one who ends up running over someone's kid.

"Night, Ms. Willet," Sandy says, then, "Thanks," like she always does. I'd like to be able to tell her things. I'd like to tell her to go away, farther than Auburn. Go states away, countries away. Go and don't come back.

I watch until she's in the house, and then I light my first cigarette since coming on to work that afternoon. The menthol hits the back of my throat like ice and I feel the nicotine trickling through me. I pull back out into the street, watchful, careful, and slowly drive toward my house on Argyle Road.

When I get to the house, I slow down to turn in the drive. From the street I can see the glow of the television washing through the windows in the dark front room. Buck's asleep on the couch, surrounded by beer cans and dirty dishes. His mouth is open, and his gut hangs out the bottom of his T-shirt. He smells like rotten cheese and drunk sweat. Some nights I'll clean up and drag him to the bedroom. Some nights I don't, and he wakes up in the morning so stiff and sore he can hardly get out of the chair except to get another beer. Not that it matters, anyway. Buck tried to hang on for a while there after Ford died, but now he never leaves the house. A couple years ago, he took all our savings and hired a Birmingham lawyer to get him declared *non compos mentis* over his depression and his panic attacks, and now he gets a disability check every month. He's trying to drink himself to death, and I don't guess I'll try to stop him.

Some nights, like this one, while I watch him sleep in the reflection of some shark show on the TV, I think, why wait? Why not go into the knives and stab him right in the heart while he sleeps? Or poison him, probably better. We aren't New York City or anything, but we've got some chaos around here. A couple years ago, a guy I went to high school with, Walker Mills, he went crazy and blew his whole family up in their rented house out on the rural route. He'd been cooking meth for years, and they said it was a lab accident, but I don't believe it. Walker knew what he was doing.

People around the café talked about it, the Mills case, all their useless opinions. It made me sick, made me wonder how they talked about Ronnie and Ford and Buck and me when I wasn't around. Sometimes I come in to work, and everyone at the counter gets real quiet. Like last year when that kid went crazy and shot up the college in Virginia, Bing's was probably the only diner counter in America where the old coots weren't lined up with their useless opinions about the deterioration of the culture. I wish they'd just keep on talking. The silence, like the silence in my house, is worse than all the wrongness there could be.

I sit and stare at Buck for a long time. My bed is only twelve steps from where I sit, but even though I've got to get up and work in the morning, I can't take it tonight. I grab my keys, slam the back door, start my car. I light another cigarette, and pretty soon I'm pulling into Cherry Street Park, where the kids still fuck in their parents' backseats. Three or four dark cars are parked out behind the ball field now. If I was to sit here and watch long enough, I'd eventually see shapes moving around inside the cars like shadowy fish in the bottom of a dark pond, see the tip of a cigarette or the glow of dashboard lights through the fogged-up windows.

One day, about a year after Ford died, I came to this park and sat on a swing where I brought him to play as a child. It was a sunny, cool morning in November, and I sat on that swing and cried for a solid hour. It wasn't the only time I'd cried since it happened. When I got the call at the café from Acie Boujean, I was hysterical. And I cried at the funeral, and I cried when Ronnie told me he was sorry. I cried when Acie came and told me he'd have to question Ronnie again. About a week after it happened, I really lost it at the café. I'd shown up to work, but Bing gave me a couple hundred dollars and told me to take some time off.

But that day in the park, when I cried for an hour in the warm sun and cool air, I knew it was different, and I still know it was different. I knew that day, and know even better now, that I wasn't crying for Ford and what happened to him. I was crying for me, and what had happened to *me,* and I've never quite been able to let myself off the hook for that.

At the end of Cherry Street, I turn back onto Rainbow Drive. I don't know where I'm going, just driving around. I turn at Sandy's street and drive slowly by her house. All the lights are out, the whole street's dark. It's late, and no matter how badly I don't want to do it, I have to go home and get some sleep. I pull down to the end of Sandy's street, a bank of grass and wildflowers that cover the barbed wire around Hank Fletcher's farm, and slowly turn my car around. I'll sit here and smoke one more cigarette. I turn the car off, the headlights too, and roll down the window, letting in the June heat. I can hear the mayflies humming in the quiet night, all the way from the river.

I smoke another cigarette, then another, sitting here in the dark, listening to the mayflies. There are other, closer sounds. The crickets in the weeds behind my car. The ticking of the engine cooling down. The sound of the cigarette when I inhale is like a tiny fuse. But it's the mayflies I hear more than anything else. I go to light another cigarette but the pack is empty, so I open the glove box for a new one. I feel my bra cutting creases under my shoulder blades—I've put on a couple of pounds. I reach around under my shirt to unhook it, leave the loops on over my shoulders. My breasts sag heavy down onto what is not quite yet a gut. I can still feel Royce's hands on them. I shouldn't encourage him that much.

I light another cigarette and blow the cool menthol smoke over my face. My other hand is back on the steering wheel now, the noise of the mayflies growing louder like the engine of a fast car, a better car than my ten-year-old Chevy. We bought this car new when Ford was five. He and Ronnie used to ride in the back when we'd go places. Ronnie was big enough to sit in the front, but Ford was still in his car seat, and Ronnie didn't want him to feel lonely. I could only see the tops of their heads in the rearview mirror as I drove, Ronnie's crew-cut black hair as black as Buck's, Ford's still baby-blond but starting to darken. Maybe Ford would have been his high school's valedictorian, maybe he could have gone to vet school. Ronnie was always a Marine—he knew he wanted to be one when he was six years old. A few good men and all that shit. Tonight, all I see is the bank of weeds and a dark, empty field like a lake beyond.

But I can still hear the engine noise, the noise of the faster car, and it takes me a moment to realize that's what it is.

Royce's black Dodge Charger, headlights off, turns the corner and parks in front of Sandy's house. He puts the car in neutral, and in the darkness of the street I can barely see, barely hear the passenger door open, barely see Sandy's dark figure get out, stand there for a moment, then lean back in for a kiss.

Then she shuts the door carefully and half-runs into the darkened carport, where the light was on when I dropped her off earlier. Royce puts his car in reverse and slowly backs up toward the corner, lights still out, then turns, puts on his headlights, opens and slams the passenger door, and peels out up Rainbow Drive.

I start my car and follow with the headlights off. There's no one else on the road except Royce a few hundred yards ahead.

The mayflies, which had been clear silver in my headlights, now look like a huge gray ghost in the darkness ahead of me. I roll up the window so they don't fly right in my car. I can hardly see but I know this road. The mayflies pock against the windshield. For some reason—drunkenness, fatigue, sexual satisfaction—Royce isn't speeding. I'm gunning it now, and I've nearly got him.

At the crest of the hill where Rainbow opens up to Highway 59, I'm right on his back. I pull the switch for the high beams and the road explodes into moving light. Royce's brake lights swerve some, his chrome bumper a blur, mayflies everywhere. Royce slows down, turns into the old Shell station parking lot.

He stops his car there. I stop mine on the road. He's getting out of his car with that tough, mean look he thinks he has, his arms all bowed out from his sides. I put my car in reverse, back up turning, and aim my headlights right at the driver's side door, right at Royce.

His eyes go from that tough slant to wide open, and he's back behind the wheel, putting the Dodge in gear when I bounce the curb, heading right at him. He floors it, and his tires spin and catch just before I get there, and all I do is clip the back end a little, send him fishtailing out onto the road. I stop just short of the abandoned gas pumps, back up, and follow him.

He's missing his left taillight, but he's moving pretty good back up Rainbow Drive, the river on our left now, the mayflies. I've got a headlight out and there's smoke coming from beneath the hood, but I'm gaining on him as we pass the mini-mall, pass the Hardee's, pass the turn into Cherry Street Park, and the smoke is coming heavier now. I push the pedal to the floor, pass the café, and I'm getting closer now, pass back by Sandy's street, where she's brushing her teeth or her hair, or she's in her pajamas or in bed or dreaming, and there's more steam, and a smell like rubber burning, and we're coming up on the turn onto the rural route where he has to slow down to make the turn and I know I'm not going to. I'm not going to slow down one bit.

When I hit the back end of Royce's black Dodge at the bend

into the rural route, the front end of his car comes flipping up past my passenger side. I swear in that instant, I look through the window, and Royce, upside down, is looking in at me, and he sees that it's me, and the look on his face is all I need. I'm ready myself now to go flipping upside down and spinning into the river or out into Fletcher's back forty or into the pines that line the road. I have my eyes closed now, and I've taken my hands off the wheel and my feet off the pedals, and I'm just waiting for the end.

But it doesn't happen. At some point I open my eyes, and I'm going a responsible thirty miles an hour right down the center of the rural route. The front end of my car is accordioned up into itself, and the smoke coming from the engine is black and thick, but somehow the car still runs. I put my foot on the brake, and I have to push hard, but the car eventually stops, and I get out and walk back down the road. I'm completely unhurt, as far as I can tell, unless I'm in shock, but then it occurs to me that a person in shock wouldn't know she was in shock, so I must have survived the whole thing.

Royce's car is wedged between two pine trees and face down in some Coosa backwater that spilled over the roadway back during the spring. There's fire glowing in the undercarriage, and both his back wheels are still spinning. This is when the car should explode, but I don't know if that's just in the movies.

When I get to Royce's driver's window, he's pinned in there something awful. He's bleeding heavily from his face, which is stove in against the steering wheel, and his upper body's not going the same direction as his lower body, and I can't see his arms at all. The car itself is bent in a V-shape, and there's no glass left in any of the windows. Royce can't talk, but his eyes meet mine as I lean in where he can see me.

"Looks bad for you in there, Royce," I say. "I'm pretty sure you're gonna die here."

I can think in this moment, but I cannot seem to feel, so I think about what I should feel, and I don't know. I think I should go get help. I think about the times I let Royce sleep with me, usually at his house, once in my bed while Buck slept in the living room. I think about Buck, and how we stayed together all those years even though we only got married because of Ronnie, and then how, years later, here comes little Ford, the boy I wanted, the boy we actually made love to make. I think, Royce is some-one's child too—but she's dead. I think I know why I did this to him, and I think it's almost a good enough reason.

I say, "If you don't die, you'd better by God stay away from that girl."

With that I turn and walk the other way down the rural route, away from my car and away from Royce, away from Buck and all of it, and it suddenly seems I may walk all night. The air in my lungs is good and cool, like I've just started to breathe again after being underwater for a very long time.

I Married an Optimist

Which is a hell of a thing to just find out, admittedly, after nearly two years of marriage, not to mention that Heather and I had known each other, off and on, for the better part of ten years. Ours was no whirlwind romance, no Vegas job, no love at first sight. We spent time, much of it alone, living in this dreadful town with few friends save each other, night after night, talking and talking. We ate our meals together, we drank our drink together, we shared our beds and our minds. Both of us wary— or so I thought—we got to know each other—or so I thought. But now it appears that the facts are uncontestable, the truth as plain as rice: my wife is an optimist.

And I want to point out that it's not merely a few good thoughts about the world, some half-assed, Christmas- and Easter-type optimism. We all fall victim to that sometimes, lose our bearings, briefly apostatize: when the worst possible scenario doesn't play out; when someone belies our initial underestimation; when we—rarely—make it to the end of a day without seriously contemplating murder. We can all get a little soft now and then.

No, I'm talking a serious conversion here, or—I shudder at the implications—a difference in my wife so profound and debilitating that it must not be a conversion at all, but must be the way she's always been. I'm talking glass half-full; I'm talking a bowl of pitted cherries; I'm talking Anne Frank here, and I don't know what to do about it.

Because I've grown fond of my wife, even, yes, to love her, over the years we've spent living this now obvious lie. I don't want a divorce. I do not want to simply throw up my hands, abandon her to the dark side. And yet, isn't it optimistic of me to think I can change her? Or that I can remain unchanged?

Because looking back, I have to admit that there were signs. A year or so ago she came home with a dog, announcing her intention to train the animal. Her quest for the tomatoes of her childhood is relentless, quixotic, Diogenesianly hopeless, and yet every time she bites into one of these measly, pesti-steroided monstrosities of today, she seems surprised and hurt by it. One recent evening, while I was drinking and sulking at the only decent bar left in our suddenly swank Houston neighborhood (the war on terror has been very good for Houston), I happened to scoff at a young woman wearing a Dollywood T-shirt. Heather proffered the opinion that the well-built and well-maintained young woman was probably wearing the T-shirt ironically, stretched tight as it was above a pair of $300 blue jeans. What's more, she proposed, the woman was wrong to mock Dollywood; Dollywood might be fun; Dolly Parton had given the wretched denizens of the previously wretched burg of Pigeon Forge, Tennessee, many opportunities for jobs and cultural exposure. I responded with my belief that Pigeon Forge is one of the major nexi of evil in this evil world and that, as chief proprietress, Dolly Parton received profit and succor from said evil, and further, that if we lived in an even remotely decent society, Dolly Parton would have never had the chance to build Dollywood, because she would have been legally put down as soon as we heard her singing "Coat of Many Colors (That My Momma Made for Me)."

"It's *nexuses*," said she.

"What's that?" said I.

"Not *nexi*. *Nexi* is not a word. The plural of *nexus* is *nexuses*."

About which, it turns out, she's right. But this, I think, is hardly the point. The point is she's wrong about Dollywood, she's wrong to bring a dog into this house and then try to train it to do what she wants it to do, and she's wrong to think that a store-bought tomato exists today that isn't absolutely putrid, and the reason is that we let them—the tomato growers—feed us this shit; it's *our* fault, not theirs, because why would anyone take the trouble to grow a decent tomato when we'll still buy the crappy ones they can make more cheaply, and buy them at a higher price? I mean, you can play tennis with these tomatoes now, so tightly packed are their piths and peels. Don't even start on *organic*. You buy that, you're a bigger fool than I thought. Organic's just a label they stick on the ugly tomatoes so they can sell them at an even higher price. Add to all of which that it should be *nexi*, because *nexuses* is too hard to say. Just try it sometime.

˅ ˅ ˅ ˅

We met in college, the University of Houston, journalism school. Old Cougar High was a pretty standard pit, no better or worse than most of the big State U's that blight our landscape with brick and fake ponds and one of each tree, but the J-school was top drawer, and it was here that I first learned the joys of cynicism. When in repose, my rounded, slightly oriental face has always tended toward a frown (my mother, repeatedly: *Try to smile, honey; you look so gloomy all the time; people won't like you*), and I found that I could use this to my advantage. I learned the easy bliss of mockery. I developed my blossoming but theretofore latent hatred of men and this world, the way you can cloak that hatred in—for you must, for it truly is—a love of Mankind and The World. I read Mencken and Dreiser and Lewis, the Holy Trinity of the Sneer, and I preached their doctrine with Pauline fervor. I wrote my early journalism pieces for *The Daily Cougar* with all the subtlety of a truncheon, but by the time I was a senior, I had honed my cynicism to a filet-knife sharpness, and I moved easily through the clammy, gray skin and the feathery rib bones of university life, straight to the guts of the stinking fish, which, in my column, The Way, the Truth, and the Right, I lay bare for the campus to see and smell.

Heather appeared that final year, trailing behind her a cape of rumor, why someone would change schools as a senior and then never want to talk about it, things like that. There had been a painful romance. She had slept with a professor and aborted their love child. She was wanted for some heinous crime. She was a drunk or a drug addict. She had gone insane.

Most of it was jealousy, the kind of petty sniping you always hear from someone's inferiors, and as far as photography went (and in most other ways as well), they were all her inferiors. By late in the fall semester, having started at the bottom of the pecking order—and never once complaining about it—Heather had established herself as our star. Day after day, her art graced our covers. The night we returned from Thanksgiving break, she first graced my bed.

That's when the talk began. Between bouts of love, we agreed on the reasons for capitalism's failure, the horrors of American culture, and the absolute slack-jawed idiocy of golf (the little hats they put on their clubs; the clothes they wear; the way they not only spend countless hours and untold thousands of dollars playing it, they then go home, sit on the couch, and watch other people play it on television, or at least they do for a while, only later to awaken with stiff necks and body-temperature drool puddles collected in the yokes of their ridiculously broad-collared shirts). We were for an educated meritocracy, the thirty-hour work week, and stringent population control. We both swore—independently—that we'd never have children, and probably never get married, unless it just seemed more convenient, for regulatory reasons, to do so.

We talked and made love, seldom ate and never slept. We didn't need it. We needed each other, our energy and ambition. We weren't *in love*—we didn't need, or believe in, that either. We simply loved. When graduation day came, we skipped the ceremony to spend one last day as close as possible without devouring each other like two snakes, and when she left to start her future in Baton Rouge, and I for a job in Dubuque, we both thought that was it.

Or at least I did. That our paths crossed again four years later seemed less like fate to me than it did to Heather. I'd taken a one-year teaching job here at the alma mater after The Failure. (Ahh, you'd know about The Failure, would you? Well, I got fired from Dubuque—and good fucking riddance to Iowa—from Augusta, Georgia—they take their golf very seriously there—and from Fayetteville, Arkansas—where I'd repeatedly made the mistake of assuming they wanted an insightful and incisive editorial page, rather than just a stroke job for the gurgly, benighted local *weltanschauung.* When you get fired from three jobs in four years, it's time to go into teaching, at least for a while, until people forget your name.) I had no grand illusions about educating the Space City's youth, but I did think that a little time away from the pinheads who run journalism in this country would be a good thing for me.

After the first day of classes, having properly inflicted upon my students my assessment of their dim futures in the newspaper business and of the newspaper business as a whole, I felt a bit thirsty, as I am wont to feel in this terrible heat, and made my way over to the student union where there was a bar in the basement that blared censored hip-hop and served Natural Light beer in plastic cups. Just as I recalled from my student days, there was a poet of some minor renown in the corner with a couple of his grad students. A few other students sat at a table in another corner trying to look as angry as possible while they bobbed their heads along to Kanye West. A bartender muscled a new keg into the cabinet under the bar.

I sat down and asked for a beer, which was soon sullenly provided by the sweaty bartender. The beer itself was sort of sullen and sweaty, and I would have left it and the bar if it hadn't been for the heat outside. No one should live in Houston in late August. It's just not worth it. I decided I'd drink my beer really fast and then leave for the day, stop at the Quick Shop for more beer, and go home and sit in front of the air conditioner and count how much money it was costing me every time the compressor kicked on. I closed my eyes to drink the beer, to pretend I was somewhere else, to dream, when I heard a voice behind me say, "Somehow, this doesn't surprise me nearly as much as I thought it would."

I didn't open my eyes. I knew that when I did, I would see her in the mirror behind the bar, and that when I turned, we'd embrace, and I just wanted to sit there for a moment more and hope before I turned and had her introduce me to her boy-friend, the poet-in-training, before I turned and saw she'd been horribly disfigured in a darkroom explosion, before I turned and saw she'd gone to fat.

I won't bore you with the reunion, the reminiscences, the reuniting. Suffice it to say she had not become fat, been disfig-ured, or, perhaps most horrible of all, attached herself in any way to the creative writing program. She was there with her ad-vertising firm, taking pictures of the campus for a new promo-tion designed to convince its target audience that the University of Houston is actually an institution of higher learning and not just the four-year dullard-storage facility the community at-large believed it to be.

We immediately fell back in as before, and within a month, we were engaged, and within three years, blissfully wed by the justice of the peace in the courthouse downtown before two witnesses who were awaiting trial for some knuckle-dragging offense. We honeymooned in Philadelphia and snickered at the Liberty Bell.

⌄ ⌄ ⌄ ⌄

But as I said, lately this inexplicable pall of kindness has fallen over our marriage. I can't even curse at other drivers without Heather telling me how it's useless and just gets my blood pres-sure up and doesn't exactly make for very good driving on my own part. This, she says, to a man who is one of the finest auto-mobile drivers on the American landmass.

We don't even enjoy my work anymore. I've been the *Chronicle*'s letters editor for a couple of years now, and I used to bring some of my correspondence home to giggle over the grammar, spelling, and opinions expressed therein. We'd drink a bottle of hock and craft responses to some of the better ones. *Dear Mrs. Jones, It is with a heavy heart that we write to inform you that your letter of October 17 was so insightful and brilliant that the entire editorial department was instantaneously struck blind by the briefest glimpse at your opinions and prose. As we cannot, in good conscience, subject our typesetting staff, let alone our readership, to such a fate, we are, to our regret,* etc. That sort of thing, just for yuks. But lately she's turned up her nose at the game, preferring instead to lecture me on what she calls "the world's misery quotient," or some such, and how I'm adding to it every day. I've advised her that one doesn't really add to a quotient, that a quotient is a product of division, and that in order to increase a quotient, one must actually lessen the divisor or increase the dividend.

"Okay," she said one night. "So which are you doing?"

"I don't even know the terms," I said. "How does one figure a misery quotient?"

"First you take all of your misery, then you stick it up your ass."

"Heather, this is ridiculous—"

"No," she said. "You want to know what's ridiculous? Ridiculous is living with someone who sucks dry every drop of pleasure in my life, who replaces it with this . . . this hate. Why do you care what people write to the paper? Be glad they're reading it. How can you go around all the time so miserable? Doesn't it wear you out, having to find something to hate about everything and every minute and every day of your life?"

"I don't hate—"

"You *do too* hate," she said, moving now from the couch and into the kitchen, where she pulled a bottle of wine from the fridge and a glass from the rack above the sink. "You hate everything but yourself, and whatever ideas you have and whatever you think is awful, which is everything, and so how can you exclude yourself? You hate even yourself. But it's not as simple as that, is it? You must hate me, too."

"I do *not* hate *you*."

"Who cares?" she said, then she looked at the empty glass, replaced it in the rack, put the wine back in the fridge. "Who cares what you hate? Did you ever ask yourself that? Why do you think everyone wants to hear your nasty opinions about every single thing? Why do you think they shut you in that room to read letters all day at work? They were sick of having to listen to you complain—they know you have some talent, and they don't want to just kick you to the curb like everyone else has, but they're sick of you. They hoped you'd get sick of it, too, if you had to read it all day long, but no, you just eat it up, like you're some kind of black hole of hatred, and you need more and more and more of it all the time in order to keep your black and hateful engine running. I'm sick of it."

"Heather, this—"

"No," she said. "I'm sick of you, black-hole man. I won't talk to you. No matter what you say, it'll only be a matter of time before you're saying something awful again."

"No, it—"

"Black-hole man. You black fucking hole. Just leave me alone."

So I did. Even though it was late, after midnight, I went for a walk among the latte shops and antique stores and boutiques that have quickly made this neighborhood "charming" in the real-estate-development sense. But this charmingness was capricious in zoning-law-free Houston, and just a few blocks from my house, I could be in exactly the kind of neighborhood I wanted, a neighborhood where people lived among one another, and smashed into one another, and did things to one another, instead of my own neighborhood, around which a hermetic seal of silence, the kind of silence that can only be bought dear, fell with the sunset every night.

As I said, it was late, which meant, unlike in most other

cities Houston's size, that it was pitch-black dark by the time I
made my way down Shepherd near the church on Westheimer.
Texans would rather have their private parts smashed with a
sledgehammer than pay state income tax, so we're relatively
free from such modern conveniences as streetlights and properly paved roads.

As I passed the old Alabama Theater to my right (it's been
made into a strip mall, Houston's architectural raison d'être),
in the dimness across the street, I could just make out Chinky
Chicken, Darque Tan, and more block-long strip malls, but unlike the Alabama Theater, which housed Whole Foods, Urban
Outfitters, and Barnes & Noble ("Barnes & Ignoble," I call it;
Heather used to chortle at this), these dim piles of cinder block
held washaterias, tattoo parlors, pawnshops, and a rent-to-own
furniture store. It was as though Shepherd was a dividing line
between real life and whatever was lived to the west, although
it was clear that before long, this line would be pushed farther east toward downtown, which itself was pushing its own
big-money Renaissance farther and farther west, planning, it
seemed, to eventually squeeze the total area of land available
to the lower-middle class into a plot the size of the average
lawn in River Oaks. As for the poor, well, no one in Houston
really considers the poor. It's *their* fault, after all, punishment
for their moral failures and low cunning. And for not learning
to speak English.

As I got to the corner of Shepherd and Alabama Street, I
turned east to cross over into the dark side, the good side. Now
don't get me wrong: I think no more of these people *qua* people
than I do of those in my neighborhood, or of you. It's just that
I admire their however diffident lack of artifice, their defiance
of the basic rules of America, whether it's conscious or not. I
respect their filth, their anger, their inability to grasp the reasons why a local-boy president, the war-on-terror boom, and
the housing bubble have left them eating Hungry-Man dinners
and driving the same terrible cars they always have. Inarticulate

they may be, but they instinctively know the truth about us as
a nation—that we are the ugliest race ever belched forth upon
this planet, that the Mongol Hordes had nothing on us for rapac-
ity, that only the weapons have changed, and that there's a
special place in hell for all of us, where we will sit counting
money all day long but won't be allowed to buy anything.

I crossed Shepherd on Alabama, made my way behind the
Thai restaurant and the washateria, approaching the Alabama
Ice House, when there in the alley behind the smoke shop, I saw
them. Three men standing over another, beating him senseless
with fists and a stick and a garbage-can lid. The men doing the
beating were young, fit, and surprisingly well-dressed for this
neighborhood, like slumming overaged frat boys or small-town
golf pros (my blood boiled). The man on the ground was obviously not one of them, was not one of anyone, merely some
poor homeless guy these schmucks decided was fair game.

I am not a violent man, never have been. But I am a large
man, with a certain amount of frame and presence, and not a
small amount of experience in the pugilistic arena. One cannot
go around talking to perfect strangers in the manner I talk to
them and not get into a fistfight on occasion.

Despite my normal proclivities to let things go as they go,
the sight of these scratch-handicappers beating this poor man
was more than I could live with. Aside from which, I can
only say that, standing there in the darkness of the alleyway,
remembering my fight with Heather, remembering that in our
neighborhood disputes are settled with writs and attorneys, I
felt some sort of kindred spirit with the beaten man, some sense
of us in this (whatever "this" ended up being) together. So I
went in, deciding, if it came to it, to hit the one with the stick
first and see if I could wrest it from his grasp in the process.

"What's going on?" I said in my most forceful voice.

"This sick fuck was jerking off in the ice house," said one of
the sick fuck's attackers.

"No shit," said the guy with the garbage-can lid, before letting the sick fuck have another shot with it. "Right in the fucking ice house."

"Here," said the third guy, the guy with the stick. "We're about done. You wanna take a whack at him?"

The man on the ground looked as horrible as you'd expect, smelled worse, and now, as he tried to roll away in the interim between blows, I could see that his pants were indeed pulled down some, that the grayish gnarled nub of a penis was indeed poking out. I took the stick and immediately split the skin between one guy's eyes, then used the butt end on another guy's solar plexus. I turned to menace the guy with the garbage-can lid, when he took a few steps back, threw the lid at me in a mimsy sort of way, and ran. I started after the first guy again, but he had risen to his feet and begun to stagger off. The man who had handed me the stick lay a few feet away, trying to get his breath.

"You want another one?" I said, feeling quite powerful with my stick and my righteousness as he rolled away. I wished Heather had been here to see it. Nothing restores a woman's faith in her man like seeing him defend the weak, and with such vigor. I had to figure the golfers would be back with help before too long, so I went to my fallen chum and said, ridiculously, "Are you okay?"

It was quite clear that he was not in fact okay, and possibly never would be, or never had been. He slowly looked up at me, bloody and toothless and old, and I saw him smile. It was an oddly unsettling experience, that smile. It created a feeling in me I couldn't place, until I realized I actually felt good. I had gone out of my way, and put myself at risk, to help a fellow human being, and what's more, a fellow human being who even the best of us would cross the street to avoid. Would a black-hole man do that?

And then the old man said, "Fuck off."

At first I wasn't sure I heard him right, through the haze of blood and the reek of booze and the difficulty in forming

*F*s with no teeth. I reached down to him, tentatively, and said, "You'd better clear out. They'll probably be back with more than I can handle."

"I said, fuck off."

"What's the matter with you, old man? I came over here and risked my neck to help you."

"You did that for me?" he said. He was clearly unable to grasp the situation. Concussion, I suspected.

"Yes," I said. "But like I say, I'm not sure how long they'll be gone. And if you really were masturbating in the ice house—"

"You did that for yourself," he said, sitting up now and pulling at his pants.

"What are you talking about?" I said.

"You some kinda angel of mercy, huh?"

"No," I said. "And it'll be the last damn time I ever help anybody."

"Shouldn't be. You here to help or get a pat on the back?"

"*You* fuck off."

"No wait," the old man said, putting his hand out to me. I helped him to his feet. From around the corner, I could hear new rumblings. They were coming, no doubt about it. "So you'll be staying with me from now on, right?"

"Look, old man. They're coming back here, more of them, and they're going to work us over good."

"What do you care? You're here to help people, right?"

"What more do you want?"

"Stay here and fight some more. I like you with that stick."

"Forget it."

"Give me money."

"I haven't got any money."

"Take me home."

"We're walking here, pal. I can't get you home any faster than you can walk there."

"No, your home."

For a split second, I have to tell you, it sounded like an idea.

That would fix her. That would flat-out fix her. You want to be good, my dear? Well, be good to this. We'll house him in the spare bedroom, and he can smell it up, and you can feed him for a few weeks until he gets back on his feet. Or better yet, we'll just keep him forever. That's what a good person would do, right? You can't very well give him luxury and then turn him back out on the street, can you? He'll be part of our family now, just like the dog, and he won't behave any better. He'll drink all day and jerk off on the couch every time you walk by. Would you do it, Heather? How much can you take? Just how strong is your love?

And then the headlights appeared, three cars and the thugs from the ice house packed in like so many angry clowns. I turned to get between the old man and his doom for a second more, to try to tell him once again to do something, run, anything. He smiled at me again, but gentler now, as if he was sorry he'd given me a bad time, as if he understood. He reached out to me, and I could see he wanted the stick. Of course. It was too late to run, and he couldn't run anyway, so he was better off having something to fight with. I nodded to him, put the stick in his hands, said *good luck*, and turned to run away.

Just as I did, I felt the stick across the back of my neck, and then my face was on the concrete. I turned to look up, to ask why, to ask something, when the old man brought the stick down again, and again, and then the rest of them were on me with fists and boots.

When I came to later—my watch was gone, I had no idea what time it was—I slowly tried to stand and was surprised that I could. My head reeled in an easterly direction, away from my house, and I saw those famous rosy fingers trying to poke me in my swollen eyes. I stood as still as possible and took stock. Obviously my legs were intact, but my ribs were hurting with every breath I forced through the blood in my mouth and throat. As I moved my arms, the skin pulled tight from the bruises and abrasions there. My head felt swollen, but I could

move my jaw with some difficulty, and if I held my eyes just
right, I could see out of the left one. So all in all—though it
was my worst beating ever—it wasn't substantially worse than
others I've received over the years. Holding my head very still,
I turned and slowly began the walk home to Heather, who was
bound to come around once she'd heard my story and salved
my wounds.

After all, I'd tried her approach, not in the soft and gooey
world of grocery store tomatoes and horn-honking abstrac-
tion, but out here in the real world, the world of fist and bone
and blood, and look what had happened. I'd been beaten and
robbed and—as the fingers of dawn became Houston's sweaty
morning palms, I could smell it, even through my broken nose,
I could smell it—urinated upon by bums and drunks and golfers, left there for dead, and what did I have to show for it but
scars? No more, I'd say, presenting her the evidence. If yelling
at other drivers got my blood pressure up, so be it. If I have
to sneer at everything, at least I won't get fooled again. If I'm
a grump, I'm a grump, or worse, and if she couldn't live with
that, as badly as I'd hate it, she'd have to take her dog and go.

After what seemed like hours, I finally made it to my corner
and turned toward the house. Heather was sitting on the front
porch steps when I came stiffly shuffling up the walkway like
Frankenstein, still holding my head at the least painful angle,
arms motionless at my sides.

"What does the other guy look like?" she said.

"Guys," I said, choking on the word and trying again. "It was
many guys."

She picked up her cell phone and called the police, telling
them I was home, that all was well, and thanks. Then she said,
"The dog ran off. I went out to look for you, and I must have
left the door cracked some. So I've been up all night looking for
both of you, and in an hour I have to go to work."

"Well, I didn't have a great night myself, exactly."

"What happened?"

I told her, told it all, the beating and the old bum and the way he turned on me, my stolen watch and, as I reached slowly around to my hip, yes, . . . a stolen wallet as well, how it wasn't worth it, how in the old days this would have never happened to me, how the world was an evil pit and everyone in it a son of a bitch, including me, but the thing is, I *know* that, and I've *always* known it, and I will *forever* know it, about them *and* me, and that if she wanted to be good and happy and love anyone but me, if she wanted optimism as a way of life, then she could have it, but she wouldn't have it and me, because I was done with anything that even remotely smacked of the milk of human kindness, and that, to continue the allusion, we'd need to stick our courage to the post and never let this happen, to either of us, ever again, and that, in fact, it was a good thing that it happened to me and not to her, the way she's been carrying on lately with the smile and the good word and the unguarded nature. She sat there on the steps, listening quietly as I said it all, looking intently at my eyes, understanding, it seemed to me. When I got done she nodded, and we sat there without speaking for a moment.

"So," I asked her. "Anything to say?"

"I'm pregnant," she said. She stood from the porch step then, moved around me and down to the sidewalk, and began to call for the dog.

CHARLIE'S PAGODA

First there'd be the drinking, then all the talk about Jesus, then around midnight the crying and repenting. I finally got enough of it and threw her out.

Her brother, Ray, and a couple of his goons came by the next morning to move all of her stuff out of the apartment. Ray was a linebacker—he'd done a hitch with the Rams, then stayed on in St. Louis to capitalize on his local celebrity by opening up a Christian fitness center, Bible verses painted on the mirrored walls, exaltation of man in God's image, that sort of thing. He has six of them now, all across the bistate region. After they were done packing, the three of them beat me up something awful, left me bleeding on the floor of my empty apartment.

I got out of the hospital the afternoon of my twenty-seventh birthday, still wearing my bloody and torn clothes. I was too depressed to go home, so I took a cab to the Grand Duck, the pub where I go for beer and shuffleboard, and where nine months ago, I'd met the beautiful, the hard-drinking, the theologically vigorous Molly.

We'd met the way a thousand couples in a thousand bars meet every night in a thousand towns, and with most of those couples it all turns out to be gibberish, much like that produced by those thousand monkeys at those famous thousand typewriters. But theoretically, of course, one of those monkeys will one day type out Shakespeare's star-crossed lovers, and there you have our story, Molly's and mine, after a fashion. Doomed from the start, so wrong for each other that, in a less muddleheaded age, our parents would have certainly intervened, even if it meant blood in the streets to keep us apart.

And our monkey script, of course, had Fate written in—the night we met, I'd just been fired from a low-level marketing job at Ralston Purina. I'd never liked the job anyway—it was just the patch I'd landed in after college, and I figured I could take a little time to find another job just as bad. When she took me back to her apartment that night, Molly said, "We have to pray very hard about this."

She sat on a hooked rug on the floor, legs crossed Indian-style beneath her in a gingham skirt I wanted to take off with my teeth. The room smelled of jasmine candles and the lights were low.

"I don't know," I said. "Is this something—"

"Shush," Molly said, eyes closed, holding out her hand to me. "Just pray."

After about ten minutes of watching this beautiful girl sit absolutely still with her eyes closed, I moved down from the sofa to sit next to her on the floor. I put my hand to the hair on her neck and gently pushed it away, and I moved in to kiss her there. She let me but didn't respond, didn't speak for a moment, until she said, "Charlie."

I stopped kissing but kept my face in her neck.

"Okay, Charlie," she said. "We can do that now, but after-ward we have to pray some more."

So we did. Then we drank some and prayed some more and made love again, and I spent the night, and that next night we went back to the Duck, and then we came back to her place and drank some more and prayed and made love again, and I woke the next morning feeling great, even with my two-day hangover. It was a clean, buoyant hangover, a hopeful one, rather than the grungy, bottomless, desperate ones I'd had for so long. So this girl wanted to pray. So what? It didn't seem bad or weird, just dif-ferent from my way of doing things. And Molly's piety was cer-tainly not orthodox. She didn't make me wait till we got married

or anything—and she did things in bed I'd never even thought
of before. As we kept seeing each other, we kept praying, but
she didn't drag me to church, rarely went herself, in fact. And
she was beautiful, and she liked a drink as much as I did. Who
knows, I thought, maybe the praying was good for me. We had
communed in word and in deed, in ritual and in act, in spirit and
in flesh. And there was a way to look at Molly that didn't make
her seem bat-shit crazy: most of the people my age were still
clubbing, playing video games all night, and Tweeting till their
fingers bled, paying no attention whatsoever to the deeper crev-
ices and spiritual swells of human life on the planet. With Molly
I saw there was this whole other side of things I'd left dumbly
unexplored. I still didn't have a job, but I did have her. About
a month after we started dating, the lease was up on her apartment, so we moved her into mine. She immediately put all of my
furniture out on the street because of its bad feng shui.

This is when the reading started. A few days after she moved
in, she came home with Cherilynn Fenster's *A Call to Nature:
Finding God in the World of the Everyday.* We read and discussed.
A week later, it was Michael Chen's *The American Buddhist:
Paradoxical Love.* Then *Religions of the Mayan World,* by Dr. Walter
Sloan, which we both found rather dry. More books followed
more weeks and months, the books' subjects running further
and further afield, until one night I asked her if we couldn't
just see a movie, just go to the Duck, just go to bed. I'd been
feeling restless lately, I guess. Molly had pretty much told me
I didn't need to look for a job anymore—she was the general
manager of two of Ray's fitness centers, and she made a nice
check—and that instead I could spend my days praying and
reading and annotating Biblical commentary and New Age
memoirs to prepare for our discussions later. What I mainly did
was drink, starting most days around noon, and when I prayed,
it was usually for Molly in the bicycle shorts, Molly in the short
red dress, Molly in the farm-girl jeans with the rip in the seat.
It had been a long time since Molly in the farm-girl jeans, so

that night I asked her, "Couldn't we just skip it tonight? Go put on the farm-girl jeans."

She set her vodka and tonic on the end table and said, "Charlie, you said yourself that you wanted to do this. I need it too, Charlie. The world gets so confusing to me sometimes."

"Okay, Molly," I said, finishing my drink.

"I'll do the farm girl later," she said. "And you can be the upright revenuer looking for Daddy's filthy old still. I'll need to protect my Daddy—we're poor and the still is the only way Daddy can put any food on the table." She slid over to my side of the couch. I could smell the heat on her neck, one of my favorite parts of her. "I'll try to distract you, but you're too upright for that, and soon I'll realize that behind my flirting and my coquettish gaze, I really do want a taste of you, you mean old revenuer with your high-flung city ways." She put the back of her fingers to my chin and neck, then suddenly turned her fingertips on me with a gasp. "You see it, too—and now there's no escape from our passion. I'll take you to the bed I share with my three little sisters, and you'll deflower me there. Afterward, I'll want to leave with you. I'll tell you everything, the where-abouts of Daddy's still, the whole bit. It's the biggest bust of your career, and you'll be famous and go to Washington, DC, and work for J. Edgar Hoover himself, and introduce your little farm girl to the world of big-time politics. But first, we need to talk about Lyman Fullerton-Hupja's *Totems for the New Millennium,* so go get us another drink."

It went on like this, more books, less farm girl, but still more and more booze. We took beer with the Bible, wine with the Torah, rum with voodoo, gin with the Celts. One night she came home with a bottle of saki and a copy of Kazumi Morikatsu's *The Maple and the Carp.* And as the months went on the talk became so much less theoretical, so much more per-sonal. She began to confess her sins to me, and wanted mine as well, although since I hardly left the house anymore except for a rare outing to the Duck, the only sin I could really think of was drinking too much. The one I didn't admit to was feeling like a kept man.

She had more, many more. She had lustful thoughts almost constantly, couldn't even pull into the parking lot at the gym without getting wet. The very smell of the place wobbled her knees. All day, every day, she plotted ways to entice one of the fine Christian exercisers into her private office. It took all of her self-control and love for me to keep her from it, she said. She went further back, all the way back, her childhood wrongs still weighing on her now as much as then, all the little awful things that kids do because they're kids and not because they're evil or bad, all the little lies and hurtful things and petty thefts she thought she needed to atone for, things she thought I could forgive. We started drinking even more, sleeping later, making love not at all. She felt too dirty, she said through the tears of repentance, felt she'd infect me with venality, her filthy mind, her ruined past.

The last night, the final straw, was when she showed up with a case of wine coolers and a copy of *The Third Annual Report of the Cyrrilean Council on Intergalactic Affairs* by someone calling herself Zulundi of Venus, a book Molly paid thirty-five dollars for that looked like it was run off this afternoon on someone's basement mimeograph. It was one thing that I would be expected to read this book and then try to formulate some sort of response that in some way connected the workings of the Intergalactic Council to Jesus and his everlasting love and our lives here in St. Louis, Missouri; I was a full-fledged exegete by now and could easily do that with any book. It was another thing that after this performance, I would be expected to listen to more confessions and wailing. But to have to drink wine coolers on top of all that was just too much. I put her and her book and her wine coolers, all three, in my car, and drove Molly to her brother's handsomely appointed mansion in Chesterfield, hoping never to see her again.

˅ ˅ ˅ ˅

But, unfortunately, here she was at the Duck, a couple of days and one serious beating for me later, sitting on a stool at a table by the shuffleboard game, talking with her hands to a bearded lumberjack type I'd never seen before. Her green eyes reflected the light above the table, her blond hair in curls lit the rest of the room. She was crazy as hell. It occurred to me, only at that moment, that that's the only way I could have ever wound up with a girl who looked like her.

I went over.

"Your brother took stuff that wasn't even yours," I said.

"Hi, Charlie," she said.

"Yeah," said the lumberjack. "Hi, Charlie."

"He even took my clothes, then they really beat the hell out of me, Molly."

"I know, Charlie," she said, crossing her legs in the tight black skirt she wore. "And for what, really?"

"I'm sending your brother the hospital bill."

"Good idea," said the lumberjack.

"So, Molly," I said. "You setting this guy up for some of your Jesus talk?"

"I'm not really into Jesus that much anymore, Charlie," she said. "I realized that you'd been hemming me in, spiritually, with your narrow world view. It's so constricting. I'm going further back. Old Testament, Zoroastrianism. It pulls everything together for me."

"That, and the Buddha," said the lumberjack, wagging a fat, red-haired finger. They clinked their bottles together and smiled.

"I'm all about taking from everything, Charlie," said Molly as I reeled with hate. "You really helped me to see that with your darkness and your patriarchal instincts. I was cutting myself off from joy. Now, I've got the East, the West, pre-Christian, even pre-Hebrew. I'm for beauty and kindness now, Charlie. Oh, Ridley," she turned to the lumberjack. "Tell Charlie what you were saying about William James."

"Ridley?" I said.

"In his seminal text, *The Varieties of Religious Experience,* William James—"

"Your name is Ridley?"

"So?"

Molly put her hand on his arm. "Tell him about William James, honey."

Ridley began again. "In his seminal text, *The Varieties of Religious Experience,* William James posits that Man labors under a misapprehension of the religious paradox and the dichotomy of the natural—"

"So this is it, huh, Molly?" I said. "This is the deal. I can't even come into my own bar anymore?"

"How absurd, Charlie. Ridley is sitting here trying to tell you something interesting. We've had our troubles, you and I, but I'm including you. It's not an either/or thing." She made a slashing motion with her hand. "It's an *and* thing." She brought her slash-hand into a plump and lovely fist. The other hand held her beer. "Ridley even has a theory that Jesus may have been Chinese."

"The other night, Molly," I said as Ridley rose slowly from his stool, "I threw you out of my apartment. I knew it would mean I'd have no furniture. I knew it might even mean a beating from your idiot brother. But I didn't think it would make me feel anything but glad you were gone. Now it does. I feel something, Molly. Before I was just tired of you. Now I truly hate you."

Ridley took a swing but I was ready, ducking it and giving Molly the full force of his lumberjack left. She tumbled from the chair, and Ridley was stupefied for a moment, couldn't decide whether to render her aid or come after me. It was all the time I needed to head for the door, my cracked ribs knifing in my side.

When I got home I opened the fridge, glad to see they'd at least left the beer. I opened one and the pop of the can echoed tinnily against the bare textured walls. I pressed the can against one swollen eye, and with the other I looked around for a moment.

Then I went back to the fridge, grabbed the rest of the six-pack by the plastic rings, and went outside to my car. At Target I bought a few pairs of jeans and some shirts, underwear, socks, just enough until I figured out how to get my stuff back from Ray. I was planning to buy a chair, but the furniture at Target was both cheap and overpriced. Instead I went by the lawn and garden section and bought a patio set, one of those plastic tables with the green and white umbrella in the middle and the four plastic white chairs. This one even had a rotating tray you could attach to the umbrella, about halfway up, for holding munchies and such, to conserve table space. On the way home I stopped at QuikTrip and spent my last twenty dollars on beer.

When I got home, I set to assembling my patio set in the living room, but the umbrella was too tall to open all the way. I took a couple of beers from the fridge and went next door to Dick Kohler's apartment.

"What the hell happened to you?" Dick said, standing in the porch-lit doorway, his back to the dark apartment inside, taking the beer I offered.

"Got the hell beat out of me the other day by Molly's brother."

"I wondered what all the fuss was."

"What did it sound like?"

"Like you were getting the hell beat out of you."

"Got a hacksaw, Dick?" I said.

"What you got to hack, Charlie?"

"Aluminum pole, about like this," I said, my thumb and finger together.

"Can I come?"

"Sure, Dick."

He went away for a moment, back into his dark apartment. Dick was forty and small, single, also out of work, always home and the home always dim, if not dark. He was a good neighbor, I guess, quiet, always up for a beer if you brought one, had tools. He was also, quite probably, the world's leading amateur authority on St. Louis sports. Inside his apartment, Dick had bookshelves filled with every media guide, every history, every program and yearbook, every statistic for every team.

"Ray did this, huh?" Dick said, returning from the gloom with a hacksaw and his can of Busch.

"With a little help from his friends."

"Ray'd hit you, if he could catch you," Dick said. "I remember the Bills game in '98, he hit Doug Flutie so hard it looked like he just swallowed him up. His only sack that year."

He handed me the hacksaw.

"But he was too slow," Dick said. "Best he ever ran was a 5.4 forty. That was in '95, rookie year. He just got slower after that."

"Yeah," I said. "I was trying to outquick them, but they sort of triangulated me."

"He's doing real well with those gyms of his."

"Hmmm," I said.

"And I hear he's opening a restaurant, family-type place. St. Louis needs more of that."

"Hmmm," I said.

"Home cooking, but healthy," Dick said.

"Let's go," I said.

The pole sawed easily, and I cut a foot or so off the bottom and gave the umbrella plenty of room to spread.

"That's fine, Charlie," Dick said, taking a seat in one of my new plastic chairs. "It's sort of elegant, in fact."

"It'll do," I said, attaching the plastic tray and giving it an easy spin.

We sat in the new chairs for a moment or two, silent, sipping our beers in the greenish glow the umbrella gave to the overhead light. We looked up at each other when we heard the tires screech outside.

And in came Ray with the same two guys from before, the three of them wearing matching black polyester sweat suits emblazoned with *Nehemiah 6:9* in a red and fiery font.

"You stupid son of a bitch," Ray said. "I'm gonna rip your fucking head off."

"*Ray Sizemore!*" Dick said, standing from his chair and backing toward the wall. "Thirty-two solo tackles in 1996, sixty-one assists, two sacks. Thirty-one solo tackles in 1997, fifty-six assists, two sacks, one interception. Returned it for a touchdown against Dallas. I saw you hit Doug Flutie in 1998—"

"Easy, Dick," I said. "There's just a misunderstanding here."

"Bullshit," said Ray. "And I had three sacks in '96."

"Well, factually—" Dick began, but Ray cut him off.

"What the hell is this?" he said, pointing at my patio set.

"What does it look like?" I said. "It's a pagoda, Ray. A temple to the shit your sister made of my life."

"You punched my sister in the face."

"Not me," I said, still sitting in my plastic chair, but slowly reaching for the hacksaw where it leaned against the table leg. "It's Ridley you want."

"Ridley?" Ray said.

"Ridley," I said. "Big guy, lumberjack, red hair."

"Lumberjack?"

"Pragmatist."

"Fuck you," Ray said. The two men with him looked down for a moment, closed-eyed, sheepish. "I told you to stay away from her, and then here she comes home tonight with a black eye talking about Vishnu and Chinese Jesus."

"There was the sack against San Francisco," Dick said, "and the one against the Saints. That was a good one, Mr. Sizemore."

"I sacked Mike Tomczak in the Steelers game."

"Oh, sure," Dick said. "That was preseason. I was talking about official stats."

"I sacked Steve Bono in the preseason. The Pittsburgh game was regular season."

"Is there going to be another beating here or not?" I said, my hand now firmly on the hacksaw's handle. I was starting to sweat some, ready to get this over with. I couldn't let them beat me up again. If they did, I was pretty sure I'd die.

"You better believe it," Ray said, and the three of them started for me before one of the other guys stopped.

"Should we beat this one up, too?" he asked, pointing to Dick, who lost all color in his face, who put his hands up in front of his chest as if to say, No, no thanks, none for me.

"Go ahead," Ray said. "But then come back over and help us with this one." Dick managed a little groan.

I let them get almost on top of me before I drew the saw. I plunged it straight into the goon's crotch, drew it back and forth hard, could feel the teeth tear through the cloth and into flesh and something harder still, like gristle or bone.

It wasn't until I released the saw that I heard him scream. He fell over into a compact polyester ball on the floor, and then he screamed again and the blood came, lots of it. The goon who was going to work on Dick came to the aid of his friend, and Dick sprinted from the apartment, shouting something about unrealized potential and concrete feet. Ray simply stood there and looked at the scene for a moment, a long moment, before he spoke.

"Jesus, Charlie," he finally said. "I mean, my *God*."

The hacksaw was still in the goon's crotch. He'd roll away from help, then thrash his locked-together legs as a muscular set, then roll up again screaming, "No, no, no!" as his friend tried to pull the hacksaw free. I picked up the only other weapon I could find, the foot or so of aluminum pipe I'd cut off the bottom of the umbrella pole. I made a move at Ray with it, and he backed up, dodging it, putting his hands up much as Dick had done, before bending down near his fallen colleague and saying, "Stop . . . shit . . . *enough*."

"Get him the hell out of here, then," I said.

"I mean, *Jesus*, Charlie," Ray said. "That was a little much, don't you think?" The man on my floor screamed, "No!"

"We need to call an ambulance," the other guy said. "He's going to bleed to death right here on the floor."

"It used to be you could get in a fight and just go home afterward," Ray said now, lost in the philosophy of what had happened, unable, it seemed, to act. "This is just so . . . *excessive.*"

"We got to get him out of here," said the other guy.

"I'm dying," said the bleeding man, his first coherent statement.

"Oh, no you're not," said Ray, who then kneeled and raised this enormous man almost effortlessly. Ray began to shout, "I can do all things in Him who strengthens me! I can do all things in Him who strengthens me!"

Ray got the man into a fireman's carry, blood now streaming down the shoulder of Ray's black sweat suit.

"I can do *all things* in Him who strengthens *me,*" Ray bellowed once more beneath the man's weight. Then he spun toward the door, then ran for it, the hacksaw still gleaming red from between the bleeding man's soaked and ruined thighs.

After I heard them drive away, I went to Dick's apartment, to check on him, yes, but also to borrow a mop, a bucket, a scrub brush, anything I could use to get the evidence off my floor. I saw Ray's footprints all down the steps, shining black and wet in the parking lot floodlights. I knocked at Dick's door.

"I'm checking," he shouted from the inside. "I'm looking it up. I'm sure you're right!"

"Dick, it's me. It's Charlie. They're gone."

"I think you killed him, Charlie," Dick said from just behind the door. I hadn't wanted to. I just knew I couldn't take another beating. All I'd wanted was to get myself out of a relationship that, mere months before, I'd hoped would never end. All I wanted was to get back to work, get my life straight again, find another girl, maybe not as beautiful as Molly, sure, but sane, or saner at least. All I'd wanted was to cut down some on the drinking, and a lot on the trouble, and to try to feel like myself again, and now I'd ended up killing someone, and I'd go to jail for a long time, maybe forever, and there was nothing I could do about it. I had no money, no way to run, nowhere to run to, and running would only make it all look worse. The only thing

I could do was try to make it all look better, clean up the blood, wait for the cops to come, and try to explain the whole thing.

"Do you have a bucket or something, maybe a scrub brush?" I said. Amid the talk of death, I didn't want to be standing out in the open, vulnerable. My ribs hurt, and I felt sick to my stomach and to something like my soul. Dick opened the door, but just a crack. I could barely make him out in the dark apartment. He wasn't looking at me, his face in profile behind the door, his head sort of bobbing up and down.

"I need to clean up this mess," I said.

"Nah," Dick said. "I can't come back over there tonight."

"Did that guy hit you?" I said.

"No."

"Are you hurt?"

"No."

"Then please come back over and help me. I'm in a lot of trouble, Dick."

He shook his head, one bloodshot eye catching the light from the porch. "I've got to get to work," Dick said. "If Pittsburgh was a regular-season game in '96, and I forgot that, then what else have I forgotten?"

"Dick, I have blood all over my apartment."

"I've got to get to my books," he said softly, bobbing his head again. "He's made me doubt myself."

"Can I just borrow—"

"Charlie . . . I'm a . . . quiet," he said now. "I'm quiet, Charlie. I just want to read my books. I need to *know* this stuff."

"Okay, Dick," I said. "I understand."

"I just need to know is all, Charlie. I hope you'll be okay."

"I understand," I said, and the door clicked shut gently in my face.

I went back to the apartment and showered, put on my new clothes, and sat at my table drinking beer and watching the blood dry and waiting for the cops to come. I have no idea what time the doorbell rang. It was late, or early. I'd fallen asleep in

my plastic chair, ten or twelve empty cans of Busch on the gory
floor at my feet. I needed to piss, figured I'd better do that before
I let the cops in and they hauled me off to the rest of what was
left of my life. The bell rang again, and then I started thinking
the cops wouldn't ring the bell. They'd say *Police!* and pound on
the door, or kick the door down, or just turn the knob and come
on through, like Ray had done earlier. The bell rang again, and
I stepped around the bloodstains on my way to the door.

And it was Molly, the troubled and variant soul, Molly in
a green wool sweater and a tartan schoolgirl skirt combo we'd
bought at the Lands' End outlet in Warrenton, boozy and bright-
eyed though bruised-eyed Molly, blond and beautiful Molly of
my destruction.

"Molly," I said.

"We're just alike now," she said, pointing to her eye.

"Sorry that happened," I said.

"Why couldn't Jesus be a Chinese *woman*? That's what *I'd* like
to know. I mean, if we're saying—"

"What do you want, Molly?"

"I heard what you did to Ray," she said.

"It wasn't Ray," I said. "It was one of the other—"

"Not my *brother*, Ray," she said, laughing. "The guy you cut,
his name is Ray, too. Ray also. But they call him Ray-Two at the
gym. The other guy is his brother, but I forget his name." She
put her fingertips to her temples. "It gets confusing," she said.

"Molly, what do you want here?"

"I wanted to see your pagoda, Charlie. Ray was telling me
about it. *My* Ray."

"How's the other one?"

"Who?"

"Ray-Two."

"Fine. Can I see the pagoda, Charlie?"

"Fine? He was bleeding pretty bad. Look at all this."

"Yes," she said, peering around me now. I moved to stay in
front of her, put my hands on her shoulders.

"But now he's fine?" I said.

"Well, he's in some pretty serious surgery right now, but just before they put him under, he said he'd gladly die for my honor. Isn't that love?"

"Oh, Lord," I said.

"Can I see it, Charlie?"

I sighed. "Will you go if I let you see it?"

"I hear it's really quite fabulous."

I stood aside, and Molly stumbled against me as she came through the door, stepping immediately into the tacky blood, tracking her size-six oxfords all through the front hall and toward the living room.

"Wow," she said when she saw the patio set. "What brought you to this, Charlie?"

"You," I said. "And Ray. I had nothing left in here."

"It's so . . . *spare*," Molly said with an inrush of breath. She felt her shoes stick to the carpet, looked down, and unstuck them with no apparent care for the reason they'd stuck. She moved toward the table, putting her hand on its plastic top, now gently gliding her fingers along the back of a chair, to the spinning tray, and then smoothly up the metal pole as high as she could reach and then back down again. She fingered the umbrella's green and white fringe. She held the handle that turned the crank that raised and lowered the umbrella. She spun the circular tray. "It's so beautiful."

"Molly, you are insane. It's a patio set from Target."

"Charlie, you should know by now that we don't always understand our own motives, or the ways beauty can enter our lives unannounced," she said, turning to face me and leaning her backside against the tabletop, her heart-bending knees beneath the plaid hem of the skirt. "Is that why you hit me, Charlie? Because you think I'm insane?"

"I didn't hit you, Molly. Ridley tried to hit *me*, and I ducked, and *he* hit you."

"Who's Ridley?"

"Oh, for fuck's sake. *Ridley.* The lumberjack. William James?"

"William James was a lumberjack?" She crinkled her nose.

"Ridley," I said, fairly screaming now. "Ridley, earlier tonight, at the Duck. Fucking *Ridley!*"

"Why are you shouting?"

"Molly," I said, "are you standing here tonight in my apartment, in Ray-Two's blood, telling me that you don't remember Ridley, that he tried to hit me and hit you instead—"

"*You* hit me, Charlie," Molly said. "But I understand *why* now. It's the same reason you emasculated Ray-Two. You're a very old man, Charlie. You have old ways and reasons. I mean, I know you're only twenty-seven—and happy birthday, by the way, I didn't get the chance to tell you that before you knocked me unconscious earlier—but your soul is thousands of years old, eons. See, you're a Hammurabian, basically, with some Shinto thrown in. That humanizes you. The thing is, Charlie, I see it all more clearly now. I understand where I fit in your spiritual and teleological structure. And I can accept that place, too, Charlie."

"I think I'm going to be sick."

"Oh, hold on," she said, quickly moving from her perch on the tabletop toward the kitchen. "Do you have any big plastic garbage bags? We should wrap ourselves up in big plastic garbage bags and turn on the shower, full-blast hot. It's not sanctified or anything, but it's the thought that counts."

"Get out."

"You don't seem to have any big plastic garbage bags," Molly said now from the kitchen, her blood-soled shoes squeaking on my crummy linoleum floor. "How about Saran Wrap?"

"Get out," I said again.

"I can start the shower anyway," she said. "We won't sweat as much, but still—"

"What are you doing here?" I said, moving at her now, tracking the blood myself, not caring, not knowing what I *did* care about. "You have ruined me, Molly. You threw away all my stuff, and then you drove me crazy, and then you got me beaten up, and now I nearly killed a man, maimed him for life, and I'm going to go to prison for it, that's for sure, and here you are again. For *what*? What else can you possibly do to me?"

"Well, when I was at St. John's earlier tonight, I paid your hospital bill. That was where they took me when you knocked me out. That's where they took Ray-Two, too, if you want to visit him. I paid both of our hospital bills. They just wanted to make sure I didn't have a concussion."

"I'll pay my own bills."

"I didn't, by the way."

"You didn't pay the bill?"

She came toward me in the hallway, holding her hands in front of her in her innocent way, then put them to my face. I could smell her perfume, her beer, her. She smiled slightly, cocked her head a bit, and said, "I didn't have a concussion."

I kissed her. You had to know I would. And I can't explain it any more than you can. But I did it, and maybe it was because she did it, and she moved her hands on my tender face and directed my lips and tongue. I kissed her neck and chin, kissed her hard, with more than my lips and tongue, with all my teeth and my cheeks and my own chin, and because now she moved my mouth upward, to the eye, the swollen and bloody eye, and she had me kiss her there, she ground her eye into my mouth and chin, and I could taste the pain there, the heat of the bruise, and because then she was crying and I sucked her tears, and because her nose ran and I licked it clean, and because we moved from the hallway to the living room, to the pagoda, to the floor beneath the pagoda, and because when we got there we were naked, as if the hands of the gods had undressed us, our clothes were things that did not exist, had never been invented, because we were clean, even in the blood we were clean and unfallen, and because we were doomed, and because we need, we so desperately need, we're so fucking lost, and sad, and tired, and when you cut us we bleed, and because if we bleed enough we die, and how, in the face of that knowledge, can any consolation we can find be wrong?

The Alternative History Club

1

I've seen him passing by in taxicabs and pausing at a fruit stand and waiting out a rainstorm in the covered doorway of Left Bank Books. I've seen him skulking into the boutiques and sneaking out of the back doors of art galleries and lurking in the darkness near the ATM. One night I saw him sitting at the back corner table, half concealed by a menu, in the Majestic Diner. I wasn't in there eating, just passing by on the sidewalk, and when I stopped and said to myself, That was him, and turned around, the table was empty. He knows how to disappear.

Although he's always different, always in disguise, and he's very old now, the eyes of David Ferrie give him away every time.

2

David Ferrie is a man of wide and varied interests. He is a pivotal figure in John F. Kennedy assassination lore, the go-between for the mob and the CIA and the far-right wing and the anti-Castro Cubans. He was a friend and mentor to Lee Harvey Oswald. He was the pilot who flew Louisiana mob boss Carlos Marcello back from exile in Guatemala. He was the guy Joe Pesci played in *JFK*.

3

"But honey, he was a bad man," my father says. "If everything you say is true, he was a very bad man."

"Popular notions of good and bad get a little fuzzy in the worlds where David Ferrie moved," I say. "So do popular notions of truth."

My brother says, "Isn't it funny how he was a fairy, and his name was Ferrie? His name was the same thing as what he was."

My mother says, "I don't like that kind of talk," but they ignore her, endlessly.

My father laughs, says, "Yeah, that's funny. I never thought of it. How come all these rabid anticommunists were fairies? You know, Ferrie, Hoover, Roy Cohn, Westmoreland."

My brother says, "Westmoreland was gay?"

"I think so," my father says. "Jill, wasn't Westmoreland gay?"

I refuse to answer. I go to my room to watch videos, either *The Men Who Killed Kennedy* or *Murder in Dallas: The Conspiracy to Kill Kennedy*. After a while, my mother comes up.

"Honey," she says. "It's okay. They just can't understand. It's very important for you to pursue this. Think of what it could mean. To everyone. To the world. But until you have proof, I'd keep it between us."

"I've told my therapist," I say. "But he can't tell anyone."

"Just be careful, Jilly," she says. She puts her arm around me, and I nestle there next to her, warm. "Don't let everyone know your secrets."

4

David Ferrie is a man of wide and varied interests. He's a pilot, a wonderful pilot—he can fly anything. He is a rabid anticommunist. He is a very serious amateur cancer researcher. He is an expert in light arms and reconnaissance. He is an outstanding magician, especially in the field of prestidigitation. He is a constant reader. He is a hypnotist. He enjoys the sexual company of boys, yes, but it isn't as gross as my Dad makes it out to be. It's not like he likes eight- or ten-year-old boys. He likes older boys. And besides, Aristotle and Plato and all those guys, they liked boys, too. So what about that?

<u>5</u>

Today I was sure I saw him near the smoothie shop on Euclid and Twentieth, coming out of the pet store next door. Buying white rats for his cancer experiments, no doubt. He wore a houndstooth hat and a blue velvet scarf, and carried a plastic bag in one hand and a hickory cane in the other. Although he doesn't really need the cane, David Ferrie is fond of affectations. I barely noticed him, but again, the eyes, black as agates, beneath the painted-on eyebrows. (David Ferrie suffers from alopecia universalis, which caused all the hair on his body to fall out. Although Ferrie initially thought this condition was a sign of cancer—he thought a lot of things were signs of cancer—scientists will tell you that the condition is genetic.)

This was the closest I'd ever seen him to my actual house, but by the time the school bus stopped, four blocks farther down Euclid, and I ran back to the corner, he was, of course, gone. This is one of the things that sucks about not having a car, even though my mom swears she'll get me one soon.

<u>6</u>

My therapist says, "Last time we were discussing David Ferrie."

I say, "Yes."

He says, "And the time before that, we were discussing David Ferrie. And the time before that."

I say nothing. I want to tell him I saw David Ferrie at the pet store, buying white rats for his cancer experiments, no doubt. But the last time I told my analyst I saw David Ferrie, he tried to talk to me about my sexual dreams and fantasies, and I don't want to discuss that again.

I want to tell him, Look, I'm sixteen years old. I get embarrassed when you ask me about my sexual dreams and fantasies. It's creepy. I don't think you're asking me about that to help me. I think you get your jollies hearing about my sex dreams. I sometimes get the distinct impression that you're hovering over me. I don't like it. You perv. I say nothing.

My therapist says, "If you don't talk to me, I can't help you."

"I think I saw David Ferrie at the pet store the other day," I tell him. "The one on Euclid and Twentieth."

He says, "I don't understand why an obviously intelligent young woman like yourself is always—"

"The one near the smoothie shop. I got off the bus and tried to find him, but he was gone before I could get back there. Which is odd, because he's very old now, and moves slowly."

My therapist says, "Last time we talked about some things you could get involved in at school. Did you look into any of that?"

My therapist wants me to go out for cheerleading. I would rather puke maggots.

I say, "I talked with Mr. Cannizaro about starting an alternative history club."

"I think, perhaps, just for now," my therapist says, "it would be better for you to *join* something rather than start something. If you join something, you can still be a leader in the context of an established environment."

I say, "Like Oswald? He joined something."

My therapist says, "Lots of other people have joined things, Jill, and it turned out fine for them."

7

I do have sex dreams sometimes, but not about David Ferrie. Most of my sex dreams are not about people, at least not people I know, and sometimes they're not about people at all. One night

I dreamed I was having sex with an alligator, and just at the end
the alligator turned into the devil. I woke up wondering about
how to tell my mother, if she'd be more unhappy about me having sex with an alligator or the devil. Then when I got completely
awake, I realized I didn't have to tell anyone about the dream.

<u>8</u>

Today at elective period, we held the first meeting of The
Alternative History Club. It was me, and Nikki Sloan, and Tiffany
Konsakis, and Rachel Weld, and Kevin Cooper (who likes either
Nikki Sloan or Tiffany Konsakis or both) and Mr. Cannizaro. Mr.
Cannizaro said we couldn't just have meetings, that we had to
have a project in order to get a grade for elective. He said he'd
leave it pretty much up to us. He said, "Just clear it with me."

Then Mr. Cannizaro leaves the room and we move our
desks together, all except Rachel Weld, who stays where she is
in the back corner of the room beneath the map of Missouri.

Nikki Sloan says, "What *are* we going to do?"

Tiffany Konsakis says, "Something easy. I *don't* have time for
this crap. Stupid elective."

Kevin Cooper says, "I got *totally* wasted Saturday night."

Nikki's cell phone goes off. She checks the number, puts the
phone back in her purse.

Tiffany says, "Did you see when Van Ramp scheduled the
SAT prep?"

Rachel Weld says nothing.

Kevin says, "I was hanging with T. J. and Sedgewick. We went
to this party. The guy's parents were in *Naples*. It was the shit."

Nikki's cell phone rings again. She checks the number, pushes
a couple of buttons, and puts the phone back in her purse.

I say, "I propose we do our project on the life and accom-
plishments of David Ferrie."

Nikki says, "Sedgewick is *such* a tool."

Tiffany says, "Have you written your essay for Carleton yet?"

Rachel Weld says nothing, just sort of stares ahead, slumped in her chair.

I say, "David Ferrie was a man of wide and varied interests. For example—"

Nikki says, "I wish *my* parents would go to fucking Naples."

Rachel Weld sighs.

Kevin Cooper sighs.

I try to think of the grossest, most salacious thing I can think of to get them interested. I think, David Ferrie used to have drag parties at his home in New Orleans. I think, David Ferrie participated in the CIA's early experiments with LSD and mind control. I think, David Ferrie made his own wigs out of bright orange monkey hair.

Nikki Sloan starts beeping. She takes her cell phone out of her pocket, texts something.

I think, David Ferrie studied the voodoo religions of the Caribbean, and regularly attended secret rites. I think, There were human tissue samples found in David Ferrie's apartment, and they were *not* his own. I think, None of this does justice to David Ferrie.

Nikki Sloan dials a number, says to her cell phone, "Quit texting me, freak."

Kevin Cooper says, "My parents are going to Des Moines this spring."

Tiffany Konsakis urgently whispers, "Bell, bell, bell, bell, bellbellbell."

The bell rings and everyone leaves.

I sit and think, New Orleans DA Jim Garrison said that David Ferrie was one of history's most important individuals.

9

"Because here's the thing, Jill," my therapist says. "Lots of people, when they've been through something like this, even long after it's over, they still have the stress of the experience. And that stress shows itself in some strange ways."

"I was never really that stressed," I say. "I know that sounds awful."

"And since he didn't have any hair," my therapist says, "and he was obsessed with cancer. I just think there's a connection here we're not exploring thoroughly enough."

"It was a long time after that I started seeing him," I say.

"Well," my therapist says, "a year or so."

"Right."

"That's not that long. The body has needs. When the body is threatened by such a terrible stress, it releases chemicals to help you fight. Your body is still in the mode of fighting. Or there are still these chemicals built up in your body that have nowhere to go and nothing to do now."

"So you're saying David Ferrie is adrenaline?"

"Not just that. Or not even that, Jill," he says. "But he's not alive and walking the streets of St. Louis, Missouri, either. That's for sure."

I say nothing until the time runs out, at which point I get up and leave.

Outside on the street, my mother is waiting. It's nice to walk home with her.

"You don't have to keep going to him if you don't want to," my mother says.

"Daddy wants me to."

"Well, your father doesn't understand you like I do," she says, taking my hand. "He thinks that it was harder on you than it was. He doesn't know how strong you are. How smart. How wonderful. He just doesn't know."

"I'll keep at it a little while longer," I say. "For him."

"You're my wonderful girl, Jill," my mother says. "Such a caring, beautiful girl."

<u>10</u>

It's one thing to assassinate a president, although it's relatively rare in the US. There have only been four out of forty-four: Lincoln, Garfield, McKinley, and JFK.

But it's another thing to get away with assassinating a president. This takes not only extraordinary planning, financing, and will, but also a considerable amount of luck. In the case of the Kennedy plot, even surviving involvement in it was quite a feat. Many, many people connected with the events in Dealey Plaza died pretty soon after November 22 of 1963. The *London Sunday Times* said that as of 1967, the number of dead people involved in the case was actuarially impossible, odds like one hundred thousand trillion to one. I don't know how to write that as a number, but it's big. The best overall count of these deaths was done by Jim Marrs in his book *Crossfire: The Plot That Killed Kennedy.* Marrs put the count, as of 1989, at 103, which is twenty-six years later, yes, but it's still a lot of dead people from a fairly small pool.

And along with the heart attacks and cancers and "long illnesses" that you'd expect, there were the weird deaths, the creepy ones, the karate chops to the neck and dismemberments and execution-style bullets behind the ear and sudden, over-whelming cancer, as in the case of Jack Ruby, the only person who we know for sure is a killer in the whole thing.

Marrs's count has forty-three deaths from "natural causes," including heart attack, cancer, and other illness. The next most common cause is murder, sixteen of them, most from gunshot, but we also find ax wounds and bar brawls and the case of mobster John Roselli, who was stabbed a mere sixty-eight times, garroted, dismembered, and then stuffed into a weighted metal oil drum and set adrift in Miami's Dumfoundling Bay. There were eight deaths ruled suicide, two drug overdoses, six "acci-dental" gunshot wounds, five plane crashes (the safest form of transport, statistically), two fatal falls, two electrocutions, one fire death (although this victim may have also been shot). One man died of surgical complications, one of a heater explosion, one of a hunting accident, one collapsed after a routine military physical. Six died in automobile accidents, four of them single-car accidents, including taxi driver William Whaley, who drove Oswald to his rooming house just after the assassination (at the time of his death in 1965, Whaley was the only Dallas taxi driver ever killed on duty).

David Ferrie officially died of an accidental blow to the neck when he lost consciousness after suffering a blackout that may or may not have been caused by either extremely high blood pressure or an overdose of pills. Despite this perfectly natural death, Ferrie somehow managed to compose two suicide notes that were found in his apartment—one was signed in his hand, the other was not.

11

My mother's leukemia diagnosis came the summer I turned thirteen. The initial odds for survival were one in five, which is twenty percent, an easy number to write. I'd see it everywhere, on the walls of the hospital room, on the bedsheets. My mother's eyes were little 20s, the palms of the nurses' hands were tattooed with 20s. I even started counting to twenty, over and over again, all day long, my life broken down into tiny progressions or interminable marches—sometimes it took forever to count to twenty.

12

Jim Marrs followed up *Crossfire* with *Alien Agenda: Investigating the Extraterrestrial Presence Among Us*, which is too nutty for words. If I start seeing aliens among us, then I'll take this delayed-stress business a bit more seriously.

13

Today I saw David Ferrie in the vintage-clothing store, pondering a pair of gabardine pants that would have beautifully matched the silver tweed overcoat he wore. I moved toward him as he headed for the fitting rooms, then ducked behind a hat tree and waited.

This was it. The store wasn't crowded. I knew if I could just wait long enough, he'd come out to purchase his pants, and on his way to the counter I'd step from behind the hat tree, and we'd finally meet, or something. At least he'd know I knew. I'd somehow make sure of that. I waited.

I would say—I think those pants will look very nice on you, sir.

I would say—I understand gabardine is a very comfortable fabric.

I would say—Gabardine was first introduced as the fabric in which the Italian Air Force outfitted its pilots.

I would say—Do you think it's possible, that if we were wearing vintage clothing, and someone hypnotized us, we could somehow channel the person the clothes belonged to originally?

I would say—I know who you are.

I waited. Finally, the vintage-clothing-store lady said, "Can I help you with something, miss?"

"No," I said. "Go away."

The vintage-clothing-store lady said, "Excuse me?"

"Would you please go away?" I said. "You're ruining this."

She said, "What's the problem?"

"I'm trying to have a vintage-clothing-store shopping experience here, and you're ruining it." I turned on her. "I thought you people were famous for never helping anyone. Isn't that right? You just stand around, and then when someone comes up and buys something you charge them too much for it, and then you scoff. Isn't that right? What's the matter with you? Can't you see I'm interested in these . . ."

I turned to see where I was, then said, "Hats," and then

I panicked because I'd taken my eye off the fitting room, and when I turned to look around the store, I knew before I saw it what I'd see. The front door to the store closing behind a man in a silver tweed overcoat, his shoulders barely visible above the racks of crap they sell in these stores. And then I tried to move quickly for the door, but the vintage-clothing-store lady grabbed my arm and said, "I demand an apology," but I pulled free and ran for the door, knocking over a bucket of black umbrellas as I passed, then out into the street and saw, of course, nothing.

I went home and cried on my bed for an hour. I had been so close, but he'd gotten away again. I cried louder now, hoping to get my mother to come in the room and ask me what was wrong, like she always did. I screamed at the top of my lungs, but this time she never came.

14

"So," my therapist says, "from here on out, no more screwing around. No more tricks, no more brain-picking, no more anything. Just two people talking. Deal?"

"I guess," I say.

"So why is it that you're obsessed with David Ferrie?"

"I'm not," I say. "I just see him around the neighborhood all the time."

"Jill," my therapist says, "the man is dead."

"I see you all the time, too," I say. "But that doesn't mean I'm obsessed with you."

"The man is dead."

"According to whom?" I say. "The New Orleans Police Department? The House Committee on Assassinations? You?"

"The man is dead."

"The what . . . the . . . the damn Warren Commission?"

"The man is dead," he says.

"The CIA?"

"Do you ever see any other people around the neighborhood?"

"You can never believe anything," I say. "No one's ever telling the truth. Ever."

"How about Elvis?" he says. "Lots of people see Elvis."

"Please."

"So you do believe that Elvis is dead," he says.

"Please. It's not even the same thing. Of course Elvis is dead."

"How about John Kennedy, then? If you can never be sure . . ."

"I'm pretty sure Kennedy's dead," I say.

"What about Marilyn Monroe?"

"Don't start . . ."

"What about Lincoln? You haven't seen old Honest Abe at the pet store on Euclid, have you?"

"You jerk."

"Why, Jill? Why am I a jerk? Because I'm tired of hearing about David Ferrie every time you walk in the door? Because I'm trying to help someone who won't be helped? Who refuses to even live in the same world as me?"

"What world is that?" I say.

"The world where when people die they stay dead."

"But he didn't die," I say. "That's the whole point. He's there, don't you see?"

"Jill," my therapist says, "they found his body. They identified it. They buried him. And they did it thirty-some years ago."

"You don't know anything about this. You haven't read the books. You don't—"

"I've read some books—"

"Some books. Do you know how many there are? Do you know how long it takes to read them all? And what a commitment it is? And the people who wrote these books—do you know the things they were up against, trying to get the truth? You don't know anything, you don't know anything about it."

"Tell me about it," he says.

"Don't you see?" I ask him. "Don't you understand that

you'll never know the truth? We're going to figure out how God
made the universe before we figure this out. The people who set
this up, you'll never know. They could release every single docu-
ment, and we still wouldn't know. We could get everyone who's
still alive to tell everything they know, and we still wouldn't
know. You could wave a magic wand and have every fact, and
you still wouldn't know it all. They killed the president of the
United States of America. And no one will ever know who did it,
or why. And to go around acting like you know, acting like Oswald
was the only one involved, well, that's the worst, because that
means you just don't care."

"What choice is there, Jill?"

"Even all these books—they look accurate, and they are
written by people who say they want to get to the truth. But
maybe they're lying, too. Maybe they're part of it. I have a book
that says that NASA conspired with former Nazi scientists to kill
Kennedy because they knew they couldn't make it to the moon.
I have a book that says the Onassis family did it. I have at least
three books about men who say they were the shooter from
the grassy knoll. I have a book that says that the Lee Harvey
Oswald who went to Russia is not the same Lee Harvey Oswald
that came back. And of course you probably know there were
lots of Lee Harvey Oswalds running around Dallas and New
Orleans during the weeks before the assassination."

"Lots of Lee Harvey—"

"It's amazing. It's something they learned about us. Usually,
you think of a plot, it's got to be kept quiet. Only a few people
can know about it. But with this one, the more people know
about it, the less we know about it. What does that say about us?
Do you realize that no other nation in the history of the world
would buy the lone-nut theory, and yet every time something
happens to one of our leaders, it's always the work of some lone
nut. The lone nut is America's contribution to political assassination. Well, again, what does that say about us? We don't live
in the real world. We refuse to. We're afraid of it."

"Do you ever see your mother around the neighborhood, Jill?"

"What did you say?"

"You see David Ferrie around the neighborhood. He's dead. I just wonder if you ever see your mother around the neighborhood?"

"Why are you doing this?"

"Just wondering."

"I'm going to say this one more time. I am not chasing ghosts around the Central West End. I do not see dead people. I see David Ferrie because he is there. He is alive."

"What happened to your mother, Jill?"

15

David Ferrie is a master of anti-interrogation techniques. David Ferrie is fluent in Latin. David Ferrie may have been one of history's most important individuals. David Ferrie, in his youth, bowled a perfect game.

16

"What happened to your mother, Jill?"

17

David Ferrie wanted nothing more in life than to be a Roman Catholic priest. David Ferrie raised orchids. David Ferrie wrote books on motivational tactics. David Ferrie wrote over three hundred sonnets.

18

"What happened to your mother, Jill?"

19

David Ferrie was a man of apocalyptic visions. David Ferrie painted desert and coastal landscapes. David Ferrie asked for the exact weight of everyone he met. Among David Ferrie's possessions were a mini Minox camera and a microdot machine. They don't give those to just anyone.

20

"What happened to your mother, Jill?" my therapist says again and again, and suddenly, as if he's summoned her, she walks into the room. She sits down on the edge of the couch and gently strokes my ankle. My therapist ignores her, says again, like she isn't even there, "What happened to your mother, Jill?" She smiles.

At that moment the door to his office opens again, and David Ferrie walks in. My therapist ignores him, too. But it's not him, not the him I've seen on the street, but the younger him, with the crazy orange monkey wig and a Lucky in his teeth, and he says, "What happened to your mother, Jill?" And then President Kennedy walks in, he's looking good, no head wound, moving confidently, handsome, and he comes up to David Ferrie, claps him on the back, and turns toward me and says, "What, erh, happened to your mother, Jill?" and then in comes Robert Kennedy, and George de Mohrenschildt, Oswald's CIA handler, and Guy Banister, Ferrie's boss, a former FBI man, and Rose Cheramie, a New Orleans prostitute who was thrown from a moving car in Eunice, Louisiana, and told police there all about the assassination *two days before it happened,* and they all say, "What happened to your mother, Jill?" and Dorothy Kilgallen, the journalist who said she was going to break the case, who was found dead of a "drug overdose" in a Los Angeles hotel room in 1965. Then Jim Garrison and Jack Ruby and even the lone nut himself, Lee Harvey Oswald, and they're all asking me, and the room is filling up now, people even I don't know, but still my therapist hasn't moved from his seat. There's J. Edgar Hoover and LBJ and Sam Giancana and Earl Warren, and they're happy to see each other, all glad hands and laughter, and all of them asking over and over, "What happened to your mother, Jill?" like it's the password for some big club, like it's some kind of big joke, and then I start screaming, and they're on me, grabbing and pulling my hair, and I'm fighting, but the whole time they're asking me what happened to my mother, and the thing is *she's right here*, with all of them, killing me, laughing, and just before I go out, I see my reflection in the teeth of John F. Kennedy's golden smile, and I think to myself that if I can survive this, it'll be a long time before I tell anyone my secrets again.

INAPPROPRIATE BEHAVIOR

George and Miranda Putnam have been called to another meeting at their son's school. It's hard for Miranda to get off work, but she's going to be there. For George, it's no problem, and there's a part of him that's glad for something to do. There's a part of him that's glad to have another grievance to nurse deep into the night. For Miranda, in this economy, this is all a real inconvenience.

Because what are they going to learn at this meeting that they didn't learn at the meeting earlier this school year, or the five meetings last year, or the three the year before that?

What they learn, George and Miranda, what they always learn, is that their eight-year-old son, Archie, is *continuing to struggle with impulsivity issues, focus problems, inappropriate behavior.* A teacher shows George and Miranda a plastic bag she keeps on her desk, filled with the work Archie hasn't finished. *He's simply incapable of completing his work.* No one says ADD or ADHD. George and Miranda have noted the way the teachers and counselors and the principal avoid those terms, probably because there are medical and perhaps even legal points involved.

"But there are some not-so-fine points involved in a word like *incapable,* too, aren't there?" Miranda asks George as they're driving home. The radio is talking about Goldman Sachs. Four soldiers killed in Iraq. "If he's really *incapable* . . ."

"You saw the bag," George says. "I don't know."

And they've had him tested, they've tried all the meds. The drugs that turn Archie into a speed freak—grinding his teeth, pulling at his hair, staring vacantly—the drugs that make him incontinent. You've got to try to establish the proper dosage, the doctors say, but George and Miranda can't stand to have Archie on those pills.

George and Miranda and Archie have seen more doctors over the past three years than a kid with cancer would. These doctor visits, with co-pays and deductibles, run George and Miranda more than $500 a month. One night, after an especially long day with Archie, George said this:

"I just, I don't know, I just think about some kid with leukemia, and what his parents are going through, and . . . I just thank God that he's healthy."

And boy, was that the wrong thing to say, because Miranda said, "Are you fucking kidding me?"

"What?" George said.

"You seriously just said that, you *thank God he's healthy?*" Miranda was sitting on the bed in a long T-shirt, putting lotion on her legs. She still had a wet little pile of cream-colored goo in her left hand.

George said nothing. They'd finally got Archie to sleep, but if they raised their voices, even a little, Archie would wake up and come running down the hall. George walked to the bed and slid his slippers underneath.

"No, George, I mean it," Miranda said. "You know what, I'm glad, too, I *thank God*, too. Because if I had to go through something like that, with you and your pious bullshit . . . You know what those parents are going through, you know how they do it? They're fucking adults is how. *Jesus.*"

"Sorry," George said.

"Seriously, you know what, I'd rather he *was* sick, I'd rather he had leukemia or whatever horrible thing you said. You know, I looked at you right before you said that, and I knew you were going to say some horrible crap thing like that. I could see it in the shape of your mouth. I waited for it. I should have started screaming right when I saw your mouth."

"I just—"

"Yeah, I know what *you just*—you think that makes it better, makes me *feel* better? You're just trying to shut the whole thing down. Ah, yes, everything's okay because at least Archie's healthy. Well, he's *not* healthy, George. He's got some kind of mental illness." She stood up to move to the bathroom, suddenly remembered the lotion in her hand. She looked at it as though she didn't know how it got there. She stopped, rubbed the lotion into her elbows and forearms.

"If he were sick," Miranda said, "there would be a course of treatment, viable options. What I can't handle is this." And she shut the bathroom door and stayed in there for quite a while.

So George has learned not to talk that way, and he understands where Miranda's coming from, he agrees that, yes, that whole line of thinking is stupid and sentimental. There's a small part of him that still thinks it's possible to recover from all this, but he can't get to feeling sorry for himself. It's going on five months, and now whole weeks go by when George doesn't have an interview. He's even started looking out of town, out of St. Louis, although so far, St. Louis's unemployment rate has stayed slightly below the national average, which currently sits at 9.4 percent. In St. Louis, it's 9.1, which means that George is not as good as 89.9 percent of the working adults in the St. Louis metropolitan area. This is one of the grievances George nurtures late at night.

And the worst thing is, he made it through the worst. Or they thought he'd made it through the worst. They'd even started to relax, or, if not relax, to grimly carry on. They started putting back some money in 2008 and 2009, when they started worrying, when people in George's field were being plowed under at a truly inevitable rate. But he survived 2008 and 2009, and in 2010 they all took pay cuts, and then he was laid off. There's an unfinished toolshed in the backyard. It has a floor, three walls, and part of a roof.

⌄ ⌄ ⌄ ⌄

"You've got to go to sleep," George tells Archie. For two-and-a-half hours now, the child has lain in the bed making his noises. Sometimes the noises Archie makes are words, the grand stories he tells himself, acting out all the parts as he fails to fall asleep. At a certain point, about an hour before he finally falls asleep, the sounds become just sounds, noises—gun noises, airplane noises, wizard-spell noises, miracles. Miranda grew up on a farm in northwestern Missouri, and she believes that the problem with all kids today is that they don't spend any time outdoors just running around on their own. They have organized activities. They have play dates. But Archie doesn't have any play dates. The doctors say a child Archie's age needs between ten and twelve hours of sleep a night, and a child like Archie needs more. They put him to bed at eight o'clock every night, and he's never asleep before eleven. Then he has to be up at seven to go to school. "You have to go to sleep," Miranda tells Archie.

When they think he's finally asleep, they'll go to close his door, and about half the time he's not quite asleep. When he's not quite asleep and you try to close his door, Archie will scream, "No!" It feels like an electrical pulse from the doorknob, straight up your arm and into a vital organ. "You don't have to scream at us," George and Miranda tell him, shaking. "We're right here. Just say, I'm still awake. Don't scream."

Once they finally get Archie to sleep, Miranda goes to bed because she has to work in the morning, and she's liable to be up with Archie's nightmares in an hour or two. George checks the ads on Monster, even though LaShonda at the outplacement agency says no one ever gets a job off of Monster. The only way to get a job in this economy is to meet people, LaShonda says. Network, network, network. George looks at Monster. He looks at hockey scores. He jerks off to porn. He e-mails résumés. The Internet costs $24.99 a month. He nurses his grievances. He reads the news. In Washington, Congress has averted a government shutdown. The deal includes another six months of unemployment benefits. Six more months? He can't imagine what will happen if it's six more months. Don't let feelings of worthlessness ever enter your mind, LaShonda says. You are not worthless because you've been laid off. There is no stigma attached to losing a job in this economy.

⌄ ⌄ ⌄ ⌄

Are you churchgoers? the doctors ask. Because a lot of times bright kids like Archie can find some sense of structure in organized religion, and moral prescriptions appeal to their inherent need for boundaries and control. Even if we don't believe in it? George and Miranda ask. Immaterial, the doctors say. So they go to church.

Are you churchgoers? the next set of doctors ask. Because the last thing kids like Archie need is one more structured place they have to go to on the weekends where they can't be kids. Archie needs that time to himself. So they stop going to church.

Tell us about his diet. Does he watch violent television programs? Does he wet the bed? How was potty training in general? Is there a history of mental illness or emotional disturbances? Has anyone close to Archie ever died, a grandparent or a pet? Miranda says no, George says no.

Has there been an unusual amount of stress in the home lately? This is where George has to tell him he's out of work. Going on five months now. The doctors nod knowingly. George wants to kill them all.

This started a long time before George lost his job, Miranda tells the doctors. George still loves her. This—when she sets the doctors straight—this is one of the times George still loves her. She's started having drinks with her coworkers after work on Fridays, and sometimes other days, too, because sometimes one of the bosses shows up for drinks, and she doesn't want to look like she's not part of the team. People are being riffed at her company, too. That's what they call it in this economy—*riffed*.

It's an acronym for *reduction in force*. A near anagram for *fired*. *Getting fired* is what they used to call it. Then they called it *getting laid off*, but that made it sound like it was something temporary, just until orders picked up again, or something, and the one thing we all know about this economy is that orders are not picking up. Nothing is temporary, except for all the things that are. Especially whatever job you find next. George has been reading about it on the Internet late at night. *Precarity*, they call it. The new economic and social reality of people's lives is *precarity*. In this economy, they call it *getting riffed*. And Miranda's been going out with her coworkers for drinks on the theory that it's harder to riff someone who's popular with her coworkers. Most of these nights cost between $17 and $25.

Then there are the nightmares. They're not like other kids' nightmares. George and Miranda don't have other kids, have never really been around other kids, but they know that Archie's nightmares are not like other kids' nightmares, because if all kids had nightmares like this, the human species would have died out long ago, because no one would put themselves through these kinds of nightmares.

Archie's nightmares—like so much with Archie—start with a scream. The doctors say that if he's screaming, he's already awake. But they're wrong. George and Miranda have stood there and watched it. Archie is sound asleep, and he screams. At the scream, George and Miranda get up, move down the hall. By the time they get to his room, Archie's kicking things in his sleep, spinning in the bed. He looks like the kid from *The Exorcist*. Then the noises start—again, not words, but noises, sometimes they're sharp little barks, sometimes they're deep heaves, like a person who's been running and can't stop. That's when Miranda and George open the door.

Sometimes that's the end of it. Just the sound of the opening door will trigger something in Archie's sleep, and a minute later, he's breathing calmly again. On those nights when Archie goes back to sleep, Miranda and George look at each other like strangers, unable to read each other's faces in the dark. Neither wants to be the first to admit how incredibly grateful they are.

Because more often, after the heaves and the kicks and the barks and the spins, more screams come. Archie is still asleep, and he's screaming with a power that starts somewhere below the heart. Then he starts clawing his hands in front of him like he's being grabbed by something out of the darkest human visions of fear. Then the thrashing, and all this time, he's still asleep, until George and Miranda go to him and wake him and hold him on the couch for two hours until he falls asleep again. Then they carry him back to bed for a few more hours until the next nightmare, and by then it's more or less time to get up and start the day.

ˇ ˇ ˇ ˇ

Touching other children. Sudden verbal outbursts, screams or shouts. Constant fidgeting. Singing. Dancing and flinging his arms when inappropriate. Nose picking. Scab picking. Fingernail picking. Talking during book time. Talking during quiet time. Taking other children's belongings. Noises. Sitting on other children. Sudden angry outbursts. Don't look at me, he screams. Whistling. Beats pencils and pens on desk. Doesn't understand no. Unreliable. Won't stay in line. Sometimes gets so locked into something there's no way to get him out. Singing and laughing inappropriately at lunchtime. Impulsive giggling. Can't keep hands to self. Interferes with other children's ability to learn. Unable to focus. Willful. Willfully disobeys rules at PE, games, and sports. Constantly acting up for classmates. Laughter incommensurate with the funny event. Has to be told over and over. Can't take my eyes off him for a minute. Never completes his work on time. Morbid curiosity expressed in frequent discussions of death. Wants always to be the center of attention. Disregards peer censure. Normal range of punishments and consequences seem to have no effect. Almost total lack of self-control. Seems to lack a sense of self. Prone to sullen moping. Takes other children's food. Cares more about what he wants than about what's asked of him by teachers. Doesn't think before he acts. Difficulty gauging risk/reward. Sometimes lashes out. Doesn't seem to see others as real people. Little sense of the future. Always says, What did I do?

⌄ ⌄ ⌄ ⌄

It's bill night in the Putnam household. It used to be sort of fun. George and Miranda would pour each other a glass of wine, toast another $385 and $312, respectively, toward their not-so-rapidly dwindling student loans, another $1602.61 on the mortgage. They'd take out a pair of dice and roll to see which credit card got the big payment that month. Now it is not fun.

The savings are what's dwindling now, and fast. They're still paying most of the mortgage, because their ARM explodes soon, and if George is still out of work then, they know they'll need all the goodwill they can muster.

They're stuck on the student loans, too—they used up all their deferments when they were saving for the down payment on the house. And sometime over the summer, they can never remember exactly when, the student loan bills are supposed to increase. In their early forties, it seems highly unlikely to either of them that they'll ever have those things paid off.

Miranda brings home $3,024 per month, except in the two months a year when there are three paycheck-Fridays in the month. This is not one of those months. George makes $1,164 from unemployment benefits.

They budget $600 a month for groceries and other household necessities. Sometimes that's enough, sometimes it's not. Gas, thirty bucks a tank, times two, times four weeks, $240. Sometimes that's enough, especially with George driving less. They got rid of the cable, the Netflix. They got rid of the Y. They got rid of Archie's after-school program, which ran them $250 a month and was nothing but a problem, since they got the same kind of calls, the same kind of trouble there as Archie had at school, even more often. Archie won't settle down during homework time. Archie has problems keeping his hands to himself. Archie throws food during Group Snack. Archie doesn't listen when adults talk to him. Archie's temper got the better of him. Archie had to be consequenced again today.

Power, gas, Internet, garbage, water, sewer, cell phone—set those aside for now. Instead, they get out the notebook that has all the medical-bill arrangements. The biggest one, the one they hate the most, is to the pediatric neurologist, a German immigrant who wanted to do a sleep study on Archie that ended up not being covered by either of their insurances, when George had insurance. They pay this man, for his *inconclusive* sleep study, $210 a month. Total up their current outstanding balances to St. Louis's medical professionals—$7,352. Current monthly payment due, $511.

Every credit card gets the minimum now, no more big payments, no more pair of dice. Total minimum payment due—$519. George and Miranda guess it's possible that someone could say there was a time in their lives that they were irresponsible with their credit, that they lived beyond their means, but really, they didn't. They both like to read books, and they bought some books. They wanted to have this house for Archie, so they bought the house. It needed furniture. They don't take elaborate vacations. They drive nine- and ten-year-old cars, a Nissan Sentra and a Ford Focus. When Archie first started school, Miranda agitated for a minivan so she would be able to take Archie and his friends places. But Archie doesn't have any friends. So at least there's no car payment.

The president gives a speech on job creation. Immediately after the speech, the Senate minority leader says no to the president's job creation plan. Republicans win the special election in New York, where a former congressman had to resign because he sent out pictures of his penis on Twitter. The stock market's

down three hundred points. In Afghanistan, seven US soldiers
are killed by an IED.

Insurances—car, home, life—must be paid, $311 per month.
LaShonda at the outplacement agency says it's smart to open
automatic payment accounts for these must-pay bills so that you
don't see them and thus they don't weigh on your mind. She
recommends using your one remaining credit card for these
accounts—she recommends cutting up everything but your oldest credit card and paying the balance in full every month. That
way the bills don't seem so daunting. George and Miranda have
not cut up their other credit cards. What if there's a car problem, a pipe break, a smashed window, a fritzy stove?

Throw the utilities back in the pile, and we're at negative $490
for the month. That's before drinks with Miranda's coworkers.
Before writing the check for Archie's lunch money. Before anything that comes up.

⌄ ⌄ ⌄ ⌄

And of course they don't need the after-school program for
Archie because George can pick him up every day. He gets
there about ten minutes before school lets out, parks the car, and
walks a block or so to the front of the school. To wait with the
mothers. They all know each other, the mothers, they're all out
talking. They're all nicely dressed. There are three categories of
mothers. The busy professional, she's on flex time, goes in at six
o'clock every morning, wears a suit, slim, distracted. There are
the rich wives, who range from the heartbreakingly cute twenty-
five-year-old to the brittle but handsome forty-something. There
are the uber-moms, thick but fit-looking, sometimes in jeans,
all with the same short haircut Miranda calls Suburban Butch.
There are no fathers. Oh, occasionally. Not today.

It's windy today, and chilly. George gets out his phone. No
messages, no texts, no e-mails. What do you expect late on a
Friday? George is sure these people, these women waiting for

their kids, are bound to have problems in their lives, too. You never know what's happening in someone's life. George waits where he always waits, by the concrete bulldog statue on the northeast corner of the school's front lawn. The flagpole lanyard rings in the wind.

And there's Archie, and yes, there's his teacher walking alongside him and holding one hand while Archie drags his book bag with the other. While he was standing there waiting, George felt that a teacher would be coming out with Archie. It was in the air, like a smell, like the wind, and so George is not surprised. What has Archie done today?

What has *George* done today? There was a coffee at the Radisson in Florissant he was supposed to attend. He didn't. He didn't even get dressed until noon. He watched SportsCenter. He watched CNN. He watched ads for injury lawyers, bankruptcy lawyers, asbestos lawyers. Our attorneys are former IRS employees, and they know how to handle your case. He watched seven-and-a-half minutes of facial cumshots and four minutes of a blonde fucking another blonde with a strap-on dildo. Two minutes of a woman fucking a machine. Less than a minute of two men fucking a woman in the ass at the same time. He checked the ads on Monster. Ignored a phone call from Miranda. Ate a bologna sandwich.

"We had just another real rough day," the teacher says. "Archie, you want to tell your dad?"

Archie does not want to tell his dad. His long hair blows in the wind. Some other kids run past Archie and the teacher and down the steps to the sidewalk. One of them bumps Archie and Archie smiles, laughs goofily, says, "What the heck?"

"Archie," the teacher says. "Tell your dad."

"I got in trouble for hugging Josh Okey," Archie says.

"Mr. Putnam, he was not just hugging Josh Okey," the teacher says. "He was practically *chasing* Josh Okey around the room. We had to put Archie outside in the hallway. You'll get a report. I had to write him up."

"I'm sorry," George says. Archie is now watching, and laughing at, some boys who are chasing each other around the front lawn of the school. George puts his hand on the back of Archie's neck, firmly. "We'll work on it. We are working on it. Please keep us informed of any problems."

"What's your schedule like next week?" the teacher says now. "I talked this over with Ms. Patti, the counselor." She says this like George doesn't know who Ms. Patti is, like he's not practically family with Ms. Patti after the last three years. "She's got some new ideas. Can we meet next week, with you and your wife?"

"I'll have to get back with you," George says. Archie has slipped George's hand, gone over to sit on the concrete bulldog like it's a horse. "I'll have to check with Miranda."

Months they've known this woman now, and she still always calls Miranda "your wife." The actual unemployment rate nationally is something more like 20 percent when you include the part-timers, the underemployed, and people who have given up looking for work.

"Mr. Putnam, the other kids have to be allowed to learn," the teacher says now, sotto voce into the wind, serious into the wind.

"We're really sorry," George says. "I don't know. I'm sorry. We just have to keep working on it."

"Try to make a time to meet next week," the teacher says. "It's important. Ms. Patti asked me to invite you."

"Okay," George says. "I'll be in touch."

He goes to Archie at the bulldog, has to do everything in his power to resist grabbing him by the arm and dragging him to the car. He does resist, and feels a little better about himself for resisting. Then he feels worse because he's got nearly three hours alone with Archie until Miranda gets home, and that's three hours if she doesn't have to go out for drinks after work. He and Archie walk through the crowd of kids and moms toward where he's parked the car. He decides he will not speak to Archie. He sets a grim look on his face. Not that not talking to Archie ever works. But neither does yelling or spanking or making him sit in the corner or not letting him watch TV or crying. They've even tried crying. Archie's maturity level is not where it should be for an eight-year-old boy, the doctors say. His emotional maturity is a little slow-developing, the doctors say. Nothing works.

They get in the car, they pull into traffic. It's about a five-minute drive to their house. After about two minutes, Archie starts singing. George looks at him in the rearview mirror. Archie sees him and says, "What?"

"Why do you do this stuff, Archie?" George says. "What is the matter with you? We talk about this every morning. You say you understand what's appropriate and what's not appropriate, and then I've got this teacher coming and telling me you're chasing some other boy around the classroom trying to hug him."

"I don't know," Archie says. "The teachers always get me in trouble. Other kids do things, too."

"We've talked about this, Archie. You're not other kids. I can't do anything about those other kids and neither can you."

Archie says nothing.

"You know you can't do that, right?" George says.

"Yes."

"Then, Archie, what the hell?"

"I'm sorry."

"Son, you can't just say you're sorry." Archie calls this *saying my sorry*. He thinks it fixes things. I said my sorry, Archie will say. I said my sorry like thirty times. It baffled George and Miranda until they realized he was confusing the second-person possessive with the contraction for *you are*. Because George and Miranda have said to him, over and over again, "You can't just say you're sorry."

"You can't just say you're sorry," George says now. "You've got to *show* you're sorry. You've got to stop doing these things you have to say you're sorry for. When are you planning to figure this out?"

"I don't know," Archie says. They've pulled into the driveway at the house. George doesn't get out. He just sits there quietly for a moment.

"Can I have a snack?" Archie says. "I'm hungry."

"No, Archie," George says. "Get out and go to your room." The house is unlocked. Archie gets out of the car, dragging his book bag behind him, past the unfinished shed. George sits in the car. The car is still running. The radio is talking about the Euro crisis. The market continues its despondent slide.

˅   ˅   ˅   ˅

When George got riffed, they sent him to LaShonda at the outplacement agency, and she explained all the programs they had available for him—severance, COBRA, social-networking solutions, job counseling, psychological counseling, emotional counseling, mock interviews. She said that most people change jobs five or six times during their working lives, and that most of the time, especially in this economy, it happens just like this. She advised George not to watch the evening news stories about the economy. She said it is very important to treat job hunting just like a job, to get up every morning, get dressed in business clothes, and get to work. She said it is very unlikely to take longer than three months.

LaShonda encourages George to recognize his own value. She says potential employers will ask him what he's been doing with his time, and he needs a sharp and ready answer. She says long-term unemployment is an emotional roller coaster. She says that regular exercise provides immediate and lasting value for the long-term unemployed. It's okay to grieve, but he won't really feel better until he gets out of his house and outside of himself. He needs to embrace the concept that change is good. Be open to starting at the bottom—once employers recognize their value, good performers are quickly promoted. She

recommends volunteering as a great way to network and con-
tribute to solving some of the problems in your community. You
need to turn negatives into positives. The fact that you've been
unemployed so long, for example—a case could be made that
this gives you a unique perspective any employer should value.
Or you could express to a potential employer that, as a long-
term unemployed person, you will be among the employer's
most valuable employees, because you now understand how
valuable a job is, and you'll work harder than anyone now that
you've finally got a job again.

Don't be discouraged by job postings that indicate they will
accept only applicants who are currently or recently employed.
Oftentimes, a third party is responsible for the job posting, and
you can turn your unemployment story into a great cover letter.

⌄ ⌄ ⌄ ⌄

Has he been checked for heart abnormalities? And brain tumors
and epilepsy? What about autism? Well, these things are
spectrum disorders. People can have them and still be highly
functional.

Tell us about Archie's bedroom. Tell us about your bedtime
routine. Tell us about the books you read to him.

How old is your house? Is there lead paint? Proximity to
power lines, to heavy industry, to busy streets? Are you on a
bus line? Have you professionally cleaned your air conditioning
ducts and vents lately? Your carpets, your drapes?

How does Archie do with various kinds of fabric? Are there
shirts he particularly likes or doesn't like? Does Archie's mood
change when he's looking forward to something? Have you
thought about taking a nice vacation somewhere? Have you
had him tested for BPD? OCD? Nasal polyps? Schizophrenia?

Are there firearms in the home? What kind of art or pictures are on the walls? Is his room on the same level of the

house as yours? Have you ever let him just cry it out? How long
has this been going on again?

ˇ ˇ ˇ ˇ

Here's something they do in St. Louis: everywhere you go,
people will invariably ask you where you went to high school.
There is a tremendous amount of data encoded in your reply
to this question, and the native St. Louisan deciphers it quickly.
Your answer not only reveals the neighborhood where you grew
up, but how you grew up. It carries with it financial, religious,
genetic, athletic, sociological, and demographic information.
When you answer this question, your interrogator believes not
only that he or she knows everything about your childhood and
young adulthood, but that they've got a pretty good idea about
what kind of person you are today. Where'd you go to high
school?

The assumptions involved in this question/answer equation
are not pretty, and to George and Miranda—neither of whom
grew up in St. Louis—it is amazing that no one ever sees how
squalid the whole thing is. St. Louisans always talk about how
hard it is to lure new businesses or new people to the area—
well, this is one of the reasons why. St. Louisans love to talk
about St. Louis as a "big city with a small-town feel," but they're
wrong on both counts. St. Louis has neither of these feels. It feels
like exactly what it is: a static, lifeless, dead-water burg, a place
that lacked enough imagination to remake itself when people
stopped using beaver pelts as currency, and that runs, after a
fashion, on the inertia of old money. Anybody who grew up
here and had any real sense isn't around to answer the question,
Where'd you go to high school, because the minute they gradu-
ated from high school, they got out of here so fast they left skid
marks. St. Louis alternates between fits of manic boosterism—
new stadia, weird art parks, frenetic ad campaigns—and long
periods of impotent civic depression. The city faces a hopeless

racial divide, a structurally unsound economy and workforce, an aging population, and hideous suburban sprawl. Every five or six years, someone commissions a massive, multimillion-dollar study to tell St. Louis what's wrong with it, why it can't attract new industry or stop white flight or revivify the schools or plug the brain drain, and then no one ever acts on the studies' findings, because it's stuff St. Louis has known about itself all along, and it's too much trouble to try to fix it. Hardly the vision young Auguste Chouteau would have wanted for his city. Chouteau was only fourteen years old when he arrived at the bluffs south of the Missouri-Mississippi confluence on Valentine's Day of 1764 to build a fur-trading post to the specifications of his employer, Pierre Laclède of New Orleans. Heading a crew of some sixty Creoles, Indians, and free Blacks, Chouteau got the post built on time and under budget, and he went on to become one of St. Louis's early leading lights. There's a street named after him, and people pronounce it SHOW-tuh, which, like a lot of things in St. Louis, is close but not quite right. Here's something people say about St. Louis: It's a great place to raise kids.

Not only do George and Miranda resent the parochial insularity of this place they wound up in, but George is convinced that his difficulty finding work is inextricably connected to the fact that when people ask him where he went to high school, he has to reply that he grew up in Alabama, moved here for work. That, in other words, he's an outsider, and in St. Louis, outsiders are weird. Also, it's pretty doubtful that any place where people go around asking each other where they went to high school can also be a great place to raise kids.

That said, there are nice parks in the area, and today it's suddenly warm. George and Miranda have decided to take Archie to the park. On the TV in the kitchen, policemen in riot gear are pepper-spraying college students somewhere in California. Without cable, the picture comes in fuzzy.

"Arch," George says. "Get up. We're getting outside."

Archie has brought most of his toys and stuffed animals out

of his room and has laid them in a semicircle around the couch, where he sits arranging and rearranging them in patterns only he can discern. The couch is not a long one—Archie can lie out flat on it, but barely. Archie has his journal with him, and every time he rearranges a toy or an animal, he makes a note. It's a Saturday. Archie hums atonally while he works, and occasionally makes a noise that sounds like a splash.

There are times on Saturday when George and Miranda can almost feel normal. But Saturdays are also a problem, because it's hard to go anywhere without spending money, and George and Miranda are trying not to spend money without letting Archie know they're trying not to spend money. Archie used to like to go to the Magic House, which is a mansion in the next suburb over that they've converted into this play world for kids. There's a pretend construction site, a beanstalk that goes up three flights of stairs, a room where kids can dress up and act out picture books, a mock-up Oval Office where kids can stand behind a podium with the presidential seal and see themselves on a television on the other wall. But for months they've been telling Archie that the Magic House is under renovation, because it would cost twenty dollars for all of them to go. And twenty dollars is nothing, of course, except three or four shirts for Archie at the resale shop, five gallons of milk, three cook-at-home dinners. So most Saturdays, especially since it's been cold, they end up just sitting at home. But today it's warm—it's like spring is suddenly coming. Strange weather. "Arch, get up," George says again. "Let's go to the park."

Archie doesn't respond. He sits in the middle of the couch and carefully selects certain toys or stuffed animals from the semicircle on the floor. His stuffed rabbit and constant companion, Mr. Carrots, is always included in his selections. Then he picks up one or two other toys, a book or two, and lies down on the couch, fitting the items around his body. After lying still for a moment with whatever toys he's selected, he sits up, puts the toys back in the semicircle, makes a note in his journal, hums to himself, and then repeats the process with Mr. Carrots and two or three other things.

"What's he doing?" Miranda says. She and George are watching Archie from the kitchen. They bought the house just before the housing market collapsed. If they'd waited a week or two, they could have probably saved thirty grand. Or been turned down for the mortgage in the credit crunch. Miranda has always wanted to close off the kitchen from the living room. Even if George got a job tomorrow, even if he got a good job, the whole first year of his salary would go to paying off debt. Their savings are gone. They cashed in his pension, what was left of it. The ARM explodes next month. George says, "I don't know."

Tell us about his activity levels. How much sugar? Sodas? Has he been checked for food allergies? What kinds of play does Archie like? What kinds of play does he avoid? What are his relationships like with his peers? How does he interact with other children?

Archie is lying on the couch now with Mr. Carrots, his Diego Rescue Pack, and two Daniel Pinkwater books. He lies very still. His hair spreads out around his head. George and Miranda like Archie's hair long, but now his hair is too long. Archie's haircuts cost twelve dollars, and every trip to the barber is a behavioral disaster.

"Archie," Miranda calls. She leaves the kitchen and goes to the couch, where Archie has sat up and is making another note in his journal. She kneels down beside the couch and says, "Archie, what are you doing here?"

"I'm trying to decide which of my toys I want to have buried with me when I die," Archie says. He says this very matter-of-factly, like this is something boys all over the world do every day, and there's something in the statement, so plainly made, that makes Miranda feel like she's been grabbed by the throat. She can't breathe. She turns to George, and he sees that crease in her face again, a line of what looks like sucked-in flesh running from her hairline to her chin. She never used to cry when they first got married, before Archie. They've fought about this. You can't lose your composure, he tells her; I have no composure left to lose, she says. Miranda sees that George sees that she's losing it again, and she hates him for seeing it, even though she knows he's right. She stands up and runs out of the room, down the hall. She decides to be a coward today. That's what one of the doctors, one from about a year ago, said to George and Miranda once—you can't be cowards with a kid like Archie.

George isn't sure what to do. But this is how it happens, how their life seems to happen these days. You wake up in the morning with a vision of the day, and in a moment everything goes very wrong. Miranda can get that line in her face and cry and run off, but George can't. So now he's standing alone in the kitchen watching Archie carry on with his plan for the afterlife.

He goes to Archie, who's scribbling another note in his journal.

"Archie," he says, "I don't think you need to be planning stuff like that or thinking about that kind of stuff."

"What kind of stuff?"

"Stuff like death. It's not good. And you don't need to worry about it. You're going to live for a long, long time."

"My teacher says people who are my age will live to be a hundred because of how good medicine has gotten. She says she'll only live to be seventy-five. You and Mommy, too."

"Me and Mommy, too, what?" George says.

"You'll only live to be seventy-five. That's only thirty-three more years."

"But a hundred is good for you," George says. "That's ninety-two more years."

"I know," Archie says. "I did the math. Want to see?"

George says yes, and Archie flips to an earlier page from his journal. There, and for the next several pages, are rows and rows and rows of numbers, where Archie has tried to figure out how many more days, hours, minutes, and seconds are in ninety-two years. Most of the figures aren't even close to accurate.

"I only have about a million minutes left," Archie says. "And that's if I don't sleep. And that's if my teacher's right about how many years I have left. She might not be right. Kids my age die all the time. They get sick or their cars crash or they fall off something."

"I'm sorry you're worrying about this," George says now. "I didn't know this was scaring you."

"I don't want to live ninety-two years. I don't want to live longer than you and Mommy."

"Look, Archie." George pulls the curtain back from the picture window above the couch. "It's a nice day. Let's get out of the house. Let's go to the park."

"Can I bring Mr. Carrots?"

"You can bring Mr. Carrots in the car, but he'll have to stay in there when we get to the park."

"The far park?"

"Yeah," George says. "The far park."

The near park is only a couple of blocks from their house, but every time they go there, they see some of the kids from Archie's class. What are Archie's relationships like with his peers? Not good. Sometimes, if it's only one or two kids, the right one or two, they'll play together okay. But if there are three or four of them, they'll gang up on Archie. If Archie's in the sandbox, they'll throw sand at him until he leaves for the swings. At the swings, they'll run in front of Archie or push him too high. On the slides, they'll climb up the ladder right behind him, crowd him, until he gets scared and comes back down, kids stepping on his hands on the ladder rungs.

The kids' fathers and mothers just sit there talking to each other. They just watch all this. They've known each other since they were kids. George just sits there, too.

But St. Louis is a great place to raise kids, so there are lots of parks. After getting Archie dressed, George slowly approaches the closed bedroom door—Miranda's in there—and he listens. He hears nothing, and he says nothing. He goes back down the hall, gets the keys from the peg by the back door. He and Archie go to the car, past the unfinished shed. George stops at the BP station and spends $13 on a quarter-tank of gas and drives into the next suburb to the far park.

When they get there, the park is crowded, but that's good, because Archie can sort of get lost in the crowd and do what he wants to do. It's a nice park, recently updated, with a new play set shaped like a mansion, surrounded by flower-and-garden-themed seesaws and swings and slides and these wobbly metal mushrooms on springs the kids can climb and balance on.

George finds the only unoccupied bench and sits down. Other parents arrive with their children, but none of them sits down on George's bench. They see other people they know, and shout hello and wave, and talk and laugh and smile, and the women touch each other's arms during conversation. It's warm, even warmer than George expected it to be, and some of the women are wearing long-sleeved T-shirts and slacks. The men, there are three of them around the playground, are wearing jeans and sweaters and golf vests and polo shirts. George tries to see signs of unemployment in the men—there's one who keeps checking his watch; George is frequently stunned when he checks his watch these days, expecting it to be hours later than it really is. There's another guy with a cell phone in a holster on his hip. If another man in the park is unemployed, George would bet it's the guy who's climbing the jungle gym and chasing two little blond girls around—overcompensating. George had planned to sit for a minute, then put Archie on the swings, but since he's seen the chasing man, he decides to stay where he is. All of the men look healthier than George—all of them are younger.

When George was a kid in Alabama, parents didn't even take their kids to the park on Saturdays. You wanted to go the park, you just went to the park. Saturdays, you got up, bolted down some sugar bombs, got on your bike and hit the streets. If other kids were mean, you just had to deal with it. You grew up, and your parents didn't have to sit there at a picnic table and watch the whole damn ugly thing. Now there are all these parents around. Spending time with their kids. Because they work all week.

LaShonda says most people get jobs because they know people who know people who are looking for people who are looking for jobs. LaShonda sends George to meet-ups, job fairs, networking groups, coffees. LaShonda says you have to put yourself out there. George is not good at putting himself out there. Even so, he can't help but feel he's worthy of a job, especially since he doesn't really care what the job is, particularly. Phrases like *working life* or words like *career* have always struck him sort of funny. He just wants a job he can get up and go to every day, get paid for, and get home to Archie and Miranda. He wants to go on vacation somewhere once a year— nothing fancy, the lake or something. He wants to have enough money to pay the bills. He wants a college fund for Archie. He likes to watch the Cardinals on television, and would like to be able to get the cable back on before baseball season. He used to buy books, but now he checks them out of the library. All these buildings he passes every day have people inside doing jobs they get paid for. Another grievance for late at night.

When he first lost his job, George would say to himself: In two months this will all be over. At idle moments like this, like sitting in the park while Archie played, George would imagine himself into that two-months-away future, and it helped him feel better. Later, when the money started getting really tight, he'd say, In two more months, this will all be over, and he'd cheer himself up by thinking about how in two months the money would seem like a lot more money because he was getting used to having a lot less. When the money fully ran out, George said to himself, In two more months, this will all be over, and he imagined himself very responsibly recovering from the long-term job loss by carefully managing his money, by upgrading his skills, by shaping his ass up. Now it doesn't even seem like he can—

Archie's nowhere. George can't find him. He was on the balance beam by the jungle gym, and then he was by the sandbox, but now he's not there. George is up and on his feet—there's a ringing in his ears. He's looking everywhere, now he's running. Out of the corner of his eye, he sees one of the fathers, the watch-checker, and he sees the man's face looking at him. George runs to the parking lot, to the soda stand. He runs into the bathroom—there are two boys in there looking at their popsicle mouths in the mirror, and when George bangs into the bathroom it scares the boys—they lock their eyes on his in the mirror before George turns to look under the stalls. "Little kid?" he asks the two boys, putting his hand up to Archie's height. The boys in the mirror shake their heads.

He's moving again—there's no telling where or what . . . there's a pond near the playground, and George sees Archie's red jacket floating in the water; the cell-phone-holster man is missing, and George sees Archie in the back of his car; there are a bunch of kids crowded around one of the wobbling metal mushrooms, and they're laughing and pushing the mushroom back and forth, and George sees Archie's sneaker pop out from underneath.

No, really, that's Archie's sneaker popping out from beneath the metal mushroom, where a fat boy at least twelve years old is now jumping up and down on top of the mushroom as the other kids keep springing it back and forth. Archie is underneath. Archie is getting stepped on.

"Hey, *hey!*" George shouts. He runs toward the metal mushroom. Some other parents—cell-phone-holster's back, there are some bare-armed women, they're up and moving now as George shouts and runs toward the mushroom. The kids scatter from the mushroom, all except the fat kid who hops down and just stands there, looking at George and another person who's behind George.

"He wanted us to do it," the fat kid says to the person behind George, who turns out to be the fat kid's mother. George has

arrived at the metal mushroom now, and he sees Archie underneath, bleeding from a cut above his eye, another on his knee.

"Lamar!" George hears the fat kid's mother say. "Lamar!"
she says, scolding. The kid's name is *Lamar*? Archie is crying
and bleeding, and George is still trying to pull him out, and
Archie screams more. His hair is caught in the metal mushroom's enormous spring, so George gets down on his knees to
lift the mushroom, but he can't lift it at the proper angle because
Archie is lying underneath. George keeps shifting his feet to try
to get the mushroom lifted up, and when he does, Archie scoots
away, tangling his hair even worse. There's blood in the dirt,
and Archie's screaming.

"Lamar, that little boy is badly hurt," his mother says now.

"Didn't you *hear* me?" Lamar says. "He wanted us to do it.
He wanted to see what it felt like in there."

"Lamar," the woman says again, and then takes the boy's
hand and walks away. When Archie sees the blood, he kicks and
rolls away from George, farther underneath the mushroom. His
eye will need stitches. Emergency room visit—how much?

Lots of parents and kids are gathered around now. Cell-
phone-holster asks George if he wants him to call 911.

"Just fuck off," George says, not so under his breath that
people can't hear it. He reaches under the mushroom and grips
the hair caught in the spring into his fist. Archie's sweating,
bleeding scalp is on one side of George's fist, the cold metal
coil of the spring is on the other, and George rips, and Archie
screams. George tries to pick Archie up, but it's hard to get
him out from under the mushroom where he's crying and for
George to get to his feet at the same time. He's out of breath
and sweating on this weird warm day when everyone should be
so happy.

"Come on, Archie," George says, still kneeling there. "You
can stand up, right?" Archie is still crying, his tears mixing with
the blood from the cut above his eye. He looks like one of those
wrestlers who's had a chair smashed over his head. Everyone,

adults, kids, are still hovering around, making it hard to breathe. Everywhere George looks he sees knees.

"I apologize, but will everyone please just leave us alone?" George says now, loudly, into the knees. "He's fine, I'm his father," George says, and feels at once that there's a failure implicit in that confession. The knees start to back away. George leans in under the mushroom where, once more, he puts a hand between Archie's hip and the gravel ground and pulls.

He's got him. Archie's still kicking and crying, but George has got him. George carries Archie to the car, has to shift him to the other arm to get the keys out of his pocket. He gets the car door opened, gets Archie strapped in. Archie cries and hugs Mr. Carrots the whole way to the emergency room, where Archie screams and fights the doctors and nurses. They eventually have to strap him down to a board to put six stitches in his eyebrow.

So the trip to the park ends up costing them $283.

∨ ∨ ∨ ∨

Today George has his first job interview in three weeks. "Good luck," Miranda said when George called her with the news. She doesn't mind working. She likes working.

There was a time, in people's living memory, when women had to justify the decision to work outside the house. Where her parents lived, on the farm in Stanberry, in northwestern Missouri, women would still have to justify such a decision, if there were anywhere in town to work. In Stanberry the only place women really can work is at the regional school, and the women who teach there are either young and unmarried or honest-to-God spinsters. Living there is like living during the Eisenhower administration.

But in St. Louis, in this economy, women have to justify the decision to stay home with their kids. And some do, and good for them, fine with that. Miranda doesn't even want that, George knows, especially if that means staying home with Archie all day.

She loves her son. She's said to George that she doesn't think she ever even understood love until Archie was born. But she does not want to stay home with him all day long.

And she likes to work, she likes her job. But George knows she doesn't like being the family's sole breadwinner. There's something wrong with that, and no rationalization or socioeconomic thinking will fix it. It's just not natural for a woman to go to work while her husband stays home and becomes less and less of a man every day. Another grievance for late at night.

But today he's got a job interview. A LinkedIn friend recommended George for the interview. LaShonda showed George how to get on LinkedIn. George doesn't know this person who recommended him for the interview, but they're LinkedIn. The guy wrote George a message, said he couldn't promise anything but an interview, but he knows the HR rep, and he'd get George on the list. George wrote him back and said thanks. The guy sent George a message: *Thanx? Thats it?*

So George had to write back and thank him more, and tell him how great he was for doing this, and how much George appreciates him and his time, and thank him again. The man didn't write back.

But George assumes the interview's still on, so he's driving out Manchester Road in make-you-weep traffic because they've got Highway 40 shut down. The radio sings, *For a hole in your roof or a whole new roof, Frederic Roofing.*

Up ahead, someone's trying to make a left-hand turn. The radio says, *Thank you and here's my address.* George is running late for his first interview in weeks, for a job he's not qualified for and that he will not get. LaShonda says never to turn down an interview, no matter what. They're good experience, and you never know. Every interview is one step closer to the rest of your life. Every interview is one step closer to the next fulfilling chapter in your life. Every interview is one step closer to the next exciting chapter in the story of your life.

And George's cell phone rings. Something happens in his

diaphragm every time the cell phone rings now. It's a whole involuntary routine. The cell phone rings, his diaphragm feels like someone's popped open a soda can in his chest, he tells himself to calm down. His fingers start tingling. He takes two deep breaths while the phone rings again, he takes the phone out and checks the number, and while he's checking, he feels this popping sound in his shoulder and neck, like knuckles cracking in there. It's been a long time since George has seen a doctor for himself. He's forty-three, a little overweight, but he did quit smoking.

It's Miranda on the phone. As George pushes the button to answer the call, the diaphragm thing starts again, because there's no good reason why she'd call. She's already said good luck.

"It's Archie," Miranda says. "The school called. Archie had some kind of freak-out. They've got him in a cool, dark room."

"I'm on my way to an interview," George says.

"Honey, I'm sorry, I know." She's quiet for a second. "I just don't know what we've done," she says.

She can't leave to go to Archie. Well, she *could*. Sure, if your kid gets sick, you're *entitled* to leave work. It's the law. Yeah, no problem, go ahead, of course. We'll just have to find a way to carry on without you.

"I'm sorry," she says again. "Someday it's going to be all right," she says.

George hangs up the phone and he's in traffic, and now he's the one trying to turn left, to turn around, and no one will let him in. Always program any contact info into your phone, LaShonda says. George didn't program today's interviewer's contact info into his phone. The radio says, *Heal your home with Helitech.* While he's trying to turn around, he's looking through all the paper on the passenger seat. Someone honks. George looks up and a woman in a blue Chevrolet is looking at him, raising her eyebrows and motioning with her hand, a cutting motion in front of her face. Go, go, he sees her mouth say. George goes. It still takes him another forty minutes to get to Archie's school. Just as he pulls up, he realizes the worst thing about all this: he realizes he's delighting in an excuse to miss the interview, and hating himself for delighting in it, which is not delightful. Luxurious, maybe. He's luxuriating in the excuse— another grievance.

"He's just having an exceptionally bad morning," the principal says, meeting George on the walkway up to the school. Someone's put an orange and black scarf on the concrete bulldog. Has he been checked for color-blindness? For light sensitivity? Two other concerned women are waiting for George and the principal in the school vestibule. One of the other women is the school counselor, Ms. Patti, who calls herself Ms. Patti because her last name is some consonant-thick Slovak impossibility. She believes that Archie needs several periods of tactile decompression during the day, so she takes him off to a converted broom closet to play with Lincoln Logs. The other woman introduces herself as Mrs. Bergeson, the school district's director of social work. The school is overwarm and there's a low-level, barely audible hum from something electric in the walls.

"Where is he?" George asks.

"He's taking a rest," Mrs. Bergeson says. She hands George her business card. "He's comfortable and fine. Let's talk a minute, and then we'll take you to see him."

Mrs. Bergeson leads George and the two other women down a hallway. A curly-haired little boy about Archie's age pokes his head out of a doorway, sees George and the women, and quickly goes back inside. A sign hangs from the hallway ceiling: *The Most Special Children In The World Walk Down These Halls.*

They go into an empty classroom. Mrs. Bergeson sits behind the teacher's desk, and the two other women quickly pull up little kid chairs and sit themselves down in them, exactly as though they enjoy sitting in these little chairs, as though they are perfectly comfortable there. George remembers the little chairs from parent-teacher conference night. He was afraid, sitting in one of them, that he'd split his trousers. He stands to the side of the desk.

"Mr. Putnam, they've brought me in from District to deliver some news," Mrs. Bergeson says now. "I'm afraid it's not good news."

There's a poster on the wall above Mrs. Bergeson's head that shows happy children, sunshine, green grass. There's a whiteboard covered in simple arithmetic. There's a bank of computers on screen saver, bubbles and waves and cosmic zoom.

"Won't you have a seat?" the principal says. She and the counselor still look concerned. George pulls up a chair and sort of squats above it, keeping most of his weight on the balls of his feet.

"This is all part of a process," Mrs. Bergeson says, putting her hands in front of her and flat on the desk in what looks to George like some sort of soothing motion she was taught in a conflict-avoidance seminar. At interviews, unless someone puts something in your hands, you're supposed to keep your hands in a relaxed position in your lap. Do not put your hands on the table. "We've been in a process with Archie, right, Ms. Kuchar?" she says to the principal.

"We have implemented a process, as you know, Mr. Putnam," the principal says. "We're just running up against the limits of that process, I'm afraid."

"Well, of this particular part of *this* process," Mrs. Bergeson says. She smiles in what seems to be a mechanical way. "And so now we need to start a new process. This is the part that's not great news, but if we think of it as a process, the beginning of a process, a series of steps, we can begin to get Archie to where we all need and want him to be."

This is when Mrs. Bergeson opens the file she's been holding, which documents Archie's inappropriate behavior during his three-and-a-half years in the school system. This is where she talks about how Archie has become an untenably disruptive influence in the classroom and how he prohibits other students from learning to the best of their abilities.

This is when she talks about how Archie has failed to respond to their interventions, and how George and Miranda's refusal to seek out appropriate medical alternatives and to ensure that Archie does not continue to disrupt his classroom has left the district with no choice.

This is when Mrs. Bergeson explains the new process, which essentially is that, starting with school on Monday, Archie will be removed from Barstow School and readmitted to Edgecliff, a division of the St. Louis County Special School District.

Edgecliff sits on Incline Road, right next to Edgemont, which is also run by the Special School District, in conjunction with the St. Louis County Division of Juvenile Justice. There's barbed wire around both schools.

This is where she talks about how Edgecliff and the Special School District have access to services Archie may not be getting at his regular school or at home. She talks about a complete battery of psychological examinations, physical examinations, psychiatric profiles, of tests, of access to doctors, of the really exciting potential of new medications. Archie will not be left behind, she says, and if things change down the line, Archie will be welcome to return to his regular school. I'm sure you have questions.

˅ ˅ ˅ ˅

How much longer can this go on? What does it mean when a mortgage is "underwater"? How long can I receive unemployment benefits? What is a payday loan? What is foreclosure? Can you be turned down for a job because of your credit? Who can declare bankruptcy? What is the current interest rate on student loans? Can a person lose their job because of a DUI? What, then, is the American, this new man? What is a title loan? What is a credit derivative swap? What is manifest destiny? The greater part of what my neighbors call good I believe in my soul to be bad, and if I repent of anything it is very likely to be my good behavior: what demon possessed me that

I behaved so well? What is a short sale? How diverse is your portfolio? How many US soldiers have been killed in Iraq and Afghanistan? What is the current unemployment rate? How can I stop my car from being repossessed? What could they see but a hideous and desolate wilderness, full of wild beasts and wild men? What could now sustain them but the spirit of God and His grace? Where does the US rank worldwide in incarceration rates? Who were the Pinkertons? What is LIBOR? What are my rights in a foreclosure? Why does the US have secret courts? What were the Alien and Sedition Acts? What was the Camp Grant Massacre? What was the Bear River Massacre? What was the Wounded Knee Massacre? What was the Trail of Tears? How shall we know when to believe, being so often deceived by the white people? How can I appeal my child's dismissal from his school? What is robo-signing? What is Intermittent Explosive Disorder? What is a junk bond? Where'd you go to high school? Why have my unemployment benefits run out? What are my options when asked to perform a field sobriety test? What is the value of a college education? What is a stand-your-ground law? How do I apply for food stamps? Where does the US rank worldwide in fair labor practices? O, ye nominal Christians! Might not an African ask you—Learned you this from your God, who says unto you, Do unto all men as you would men should do unto you? Is it not enough that we are torn from our country and friends, to toil for your luxury and lust of gain? Must every tender feeling likewise be sacrificed to your avarice? Why does an American CEO earn 350 times the salary of the average worker? Because that's what the market will bear? What are we going to do? If my child's new school doesn't notice that his classmates have locked him in a broom closet for three hours, does that constitute neglect? Does nobody know poor Rip Van Winkle? What are the effects of homelessness on children? What happens if I default on my student loans? Where does the US rank worldwide in income inequality? What is a hedge fund? Why does a Nobel Peace

Prize winner have a "kill list"? What is a right-to-work state? If you haven't heard my personal, guaranteed secret for safely and legally building your wealth while paying off your debts at pennies on the dollar, what are you waiting for? What would we really know the meaning of? Do you guess I have some intricate purpose? Where does the US rank worldwide in the cost of medical care? How many drinks would it take a 128-pound woman to reach the legal blood alcohol limit in Missouri? How do I apply for Medicaid? Can we get you set up in a payment plan today? What is Section 8 housing? What is peonage? What is HAMP? What is HARP? What is TARP? Where'd you go to high school? What is the three-fifths clause? What was the Missouri Compromise? What to the American slave is your fourth of July? What was the Dred Scott decision? Is this the little woman who made the great war? Why are we so alone? What are the housing options for people who've declared bankruptcy? Who were the robber barons? What is the US's largest private employer? How many Americans are killed by terrorists each year? By guns? What is American exceptionalism? What was the Ludlow Massacre? Where does the US rank worldwide in income tax rates? What is wage garnishment? How long does COBRA last? What is General Anxiety Disorder? How can I disappear completely? What was the Gilded Age? Where does the US rank worldwide in the quality of its infrastructure? What is the current unemployment rate? Now, because this is the great inquiry of all men: what Indians have been converted? What have the English done in those parts? What was the Bisbee Deportation? What was the Columbine Massacre? What was the Columbine Mine Massacre? What is being done in our names? Are you saving enough for retirement? How many guns are there in the US? Who were Sacco and Vanzetti? How does one "walk" on an "underwater" mortgage? Do you just pack up and leave? Where do you go? Three hours, and no one noticed he was missing? What if I can't afford a lawyer? What was the Wartime Civilian Control Agency?

Why are they tear-gassing college students? When did the 2008 recession officially end? What was the cost of the wars in Iraq and Afghanistan? What was the Triangle Shirtwaist Factory Fire? What was the Red Scare? Then straight I 'gin my heart to chide, And did thy wealth on earth abide? Where'd you go to high school? What is going to happen? Where are the weapons of mass destruction? What is the suicide rate in the US armed forces? What is enhanced interrogation? Why should there not be a patient confidence in the ultimate justice of the people? Is there any better or equal hope in the world? What was the Citizens United decision? Where does the US rank worldwide in economic and social mobility? How can I get help paying for my child's medications? How many guns does the US export each year? What is mortgage securitization? Why haven't we closed Guantánamo? Is Missouri a no-fault divorce state? How do you ask a man to be the last man to die for a mistake? Who are the 1 percent? Have you, at long last, no sense of decency, sir? What are my rights as a patient? Is your money working hard enough for you? Do suicide rates rise during a depression? Why exactly did we go to war in Iraq? How does it become a man to behave toward this American government today? What is the greatest country in the world? What is the current unemployment rate? Where does the US rank world-wide in education? What is Post-Traumatic Stress Disorder? What if I owe more in taxes than I can pay? Would you have me argue that man is entitled to liberty? How secure is your nest egg? What is the frame of government under which we live? What is Avoidant Personality Disorder? The first question I am tempted to put to the proprietor of such impropriety is, Who bolsters you? Are you one of the ninety-seven who fail? or of the three who succeed? What is the American Dream? What *can* you afford to pay? O! then, what will be the consequences? What will become of the poor worms that shall suffer it? Whose hands can be strong? And whose heart can endure? Don't you have any friends or family who could help you out, just till you

get over the hump? What are we going to do? What do you
expect us to do? Shouldn't somebody do something about this?
Is there then no superintending power who conducts the moral
operations of the world, as well as the physical? The same sub-
lime hand which guides the planets round the sun with so much
exactness, which preserves the arrangement of the whole with
such exalted wisdom and paternal care, and prevents the vast
system from falling into confusion; doth it abandon mankind
to all the errors, the follies, and the miseries, which their most
frantic rage, and their most dangerous vices and passions can
produce? Can you hear me now? What are futures? Where'd
you go to high school?

v v v v

Once upon a time, there was a man. He lived with his wife and
his son in what he'd always been told was the greatest country in the world. God-loved and manifest. A city upon a hill.
Commensurate to his capacity for wonder. The last, best hope
of Earth. Then when the man reached what should have been
his happiest and safest and most productive years, everything
went wrong.

The man lost his job and he couldn't find another one. The
wife didn't make enough money to support the family by herself. The son needed expensive doctors. The man and his family
lost their home. They were very poor now, and because they
were so poor it was hard to find another place to live, and it was
hard to find a place for the boy to go to school. They knew that
around the country, a whole lot of people had things happening
to them that were even worse. But that didn't help. Their lives
were panic. Everything was very bad.

Sometimes the man would say, "What happened?" Sometimes the wife would say, "What are we going to do?" Sometimes
one or the other of them would say, "Things *have* to get better."
After a while, they pretty much just stared at each other across

the tiny apartment they'd moved into. Until things got better, until they figured out what to do, until something happened, there wasn't really much to say. Neither of them could remember the last time they'd really talked, held hands, touched.

Their son watched all of this, and he was a smart boy. Everyone thought he was stupid, but he wasn't. He didn't understand why everyone thought he was stupid, but it didn't matter, because he knew he wasn't. The boy watched his parents. He knew they were scared. But the boy was not scared.

The boy got Mr. Carrots when he was five and they still lived in the house. The boy liked sleeping on the couch in the new apartment. His father would sit in the chair next to the couch while the boy fell asleep. His mother hated the kitchen. "I hate this kitchen," his mother said. There was a corner of the kitchen floor that was curled up and underneath it was dirty and gross. There was also a hole in the wall where the doorknob hit it. And he slept with Mr. Carrots on the couch.

But aside from sleeping on the couch, the boy didn't like anything about the apartment complex. There were other kids who lived there, and they were all mean to him, and he didn't have his own room. And his father wouldn't ever let him go outside and play by himself, because there were bad people in the neighborhood, "and we have to live here for a little while, so we just have to be careful." And when the boy went outside to play, the father always came along, because the father was scared. But the boy was not scared.

One day the boy's father got a phone call. The boy was playing Mario, but it was hard to play on the new TV because the screen was smaller and Mario didn't fit all the way. Sometimes he'd disappear completely off the edge of the screen. Sometimes the boy would move Mario over to the edge of the screen and make him disappear and come back, disappear and come back, disappear and come back, disappear and come back.

So the father said to the boy, "I have to go out. Stay inside, and do not open the door for anybody ever at all under any circumstances. Don't be scared." The boy was not scared. The father was walking very fast, getting his clothes on and making sure things like the coffee maker were turned off. The air started making funny noises, and the boy tried a quiet spell, but it didn't work because his father was still there. The boy had never been left alone before, but he could fly and he could turn himself invisible and he could go through walls if his father wasn't there, which was something else they didn't know about him. The father took the boy to the phone and made sure the boy knew the numbers. The boy knew the numbers. He went and got Mr. Carrots and sat back down in front of the little TV. Mr. Carrots still had a bloodstain on his forehead from the time they lost the battle at the far park, but he was okay now.

Everybody thought the boy was stupid, they'd say it all the time, stupid stupid stupid. Kids said that. But he wasn't stupid, and it hurt his feelings. His parents and his teachers from when he went to school, they said, You've got to pay attention, which felt a little bit like another way to say stupid. But he was paying attention. He heard everything they said. And he didn't understand why people didn't understand that he was just happy.

"Here's a clock," the boy's father said. He was wearing his suit and sweating, and he smelled like something gross in the backyard that the boy found when they had a backyard. It was something that had died and didn't have any skin left on it. His grandparents also had all died, and he could remember only one of them, from that time they went to the farm and he won a lot of battles there.

His father raised two fingers and said, "I'll be back in two hours. Do you know when two hours will be?" The boy nodded. He wanted to correct the way his father said the question, because it didn't make any sense, but his father said, "Don't be scared," but the boy wasn't scared because he had a sword too, and his father said, "Don't answer the phone, stay away from the windows, and don't open that door. Do you understand? Just stay right here with Mr. Carrots and play Mario." The boy nodded.

When the father locked the door, the boy went to the window. As soon as the father got in his car, a monster picked up his car and threw it all the way to where the boy couldn't see. The boy got his sword and Mr. Carrots got his laser, and the boy said the spell to go through the door so they could rescue the apartment complex. Then they killed the monster. Then later they flew to a distant land on the other side of the world and found his father there, but his father didn't want to come back because he had a whole new family and a job and he was scared of coming back home. "I have to stay here," his father said. "I'm really sorry. I love you, but I won't see you anymore." Then Mr. Carrots said to the boy, "You have to save America! Look! It's an emergency!"

And the boy looked back at America, and there were more monsters and vampires and space aliens, and the boy and Mr. Carrots helped the army kill the monsters that were attacking America. When all the monsters were dead, they made a movie about the boy and Mr. Carrots. Then the boy became the president. He made a law that all fathers could have jobs. He gave a speech and told everyone to be nice to each other, and be friends, and help each other with things. And everybody did. When he knew it was safe, the boy sent a message to his father, and his father came home and got a job and lived in the old house with the boy's mother.

And the boy was the president for ninety-two years, and the people of America lived happily ever after.

Acknowledgments

These stories have been published, sometimes in a different form, in the following publications: "The Passage" in *The Missouri Review*; "Ready for Schmelling" in *Phoebe*; "Lubbock Is Not a Place of the Spirit" in *Epoch* and in *The Road to Nowhere and Other New Stories from the Southwest* (University of New Mexico Press, 2013); "The Thing about Norfolk" in *The Normal School*; "I Married an Optimist" in *Low Rent*; "Charlie's Pagoda" in *Roanoke Review*; and "The Alternative History Club" in *Black Warrior Review*.

So many friends, family members, teachers, colleagues, and other writers have helped to make this book better. You know who you are, or you will know who you are next time I see you. Fair warning.

Special thanks to Daniel Slager and everyone at Milkweed Editions; to my agent, Renee Zuckerbrot and her assistant, Anne Horowitz; to Marc McKee, who they're never gonna catch, because he's fucking innocent; to Wayne Miller, who holds the naming rights for all my future work; and to the absolutely, positively indispensable Brian Barker.

And most of all, to David Clewell.

Just in case the lines in "Lubbock Is Not a Place of the Spirit" that were lifted from the 1976 film *Taxi Driver* (Martin Scorsese, director; Paul Schrader, writer) do not, to some readers, appear in their proper light of homage, please be assured that homage was the intent.

While this story collection occasionally makes fictional use of characters who share the names and some attributes of people who once lived, any innocent bystanders to the events recorded herein have either had their names changed or are products of the author's mere imagination.

MURRAY FARISH'S short stories have appeared in *The Missouri Review*, *Epoch*, *Roanoke Review*, and *Black Warrior Review*, among other publications. His work has been awarded the William Peden Prize, the Phoebe Fiction Prize, and the Donald Barthelme Memorial Fellowship Prize. Farish lives with his wife and two sons in St. Louis, Missouri, where he teaches writing and literature at Webster University. *Inappropriate Behavior* is his first book.

Interior design by Connie Kuhnz
Typeset in Baskerville MT
by BookMobile Design & Digital Publisher Services